Spare the Rod

The fourth book of Sherborne medieval mysteries

By

Rosie Lear

Grosvenor House
Publishing Limited

This book is published by
Grosvenor House Publishing Ltd
Link House
140 The Broadway, Tolworth, Surrey, KT6 7HT.
www.grosvenorhousepublishing.co.uk

This book is a work of fiction. Any resemblance to
people or events, past or present, is purely coincidental.

A CIP record for this book
is available from the British Library

ISBN 978-1-83975-197-4

rosielearbooks.com

For Maria Winter and David Burke,
followers of Matthias from the beginning.

MATTHIAS' JOURNEY

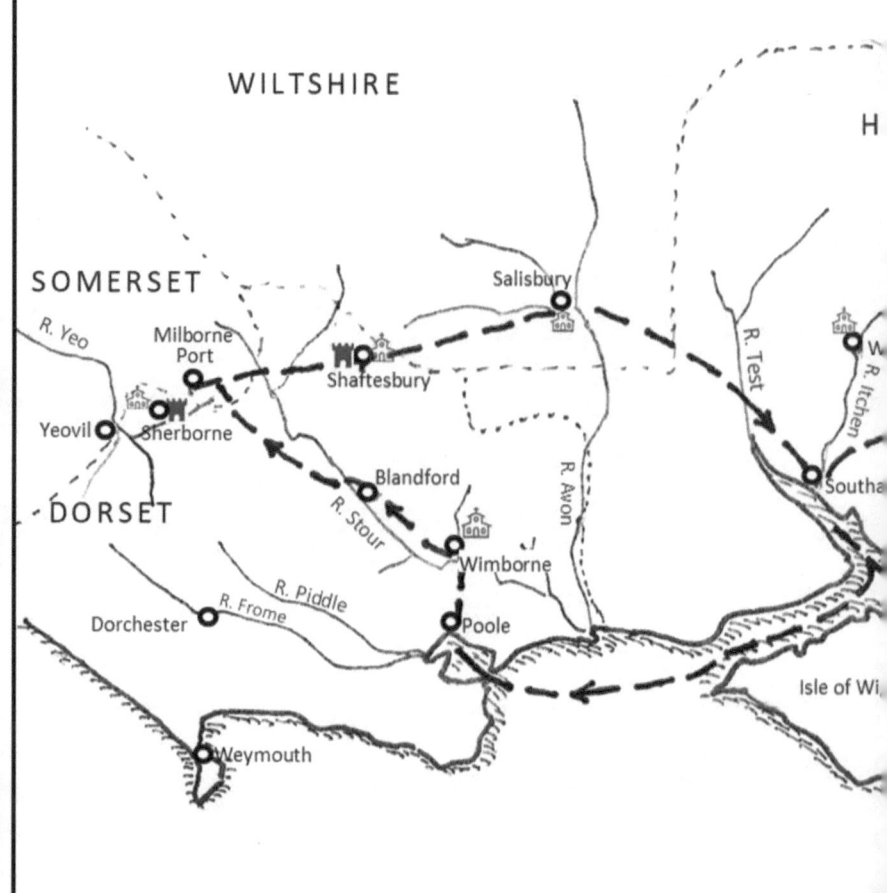

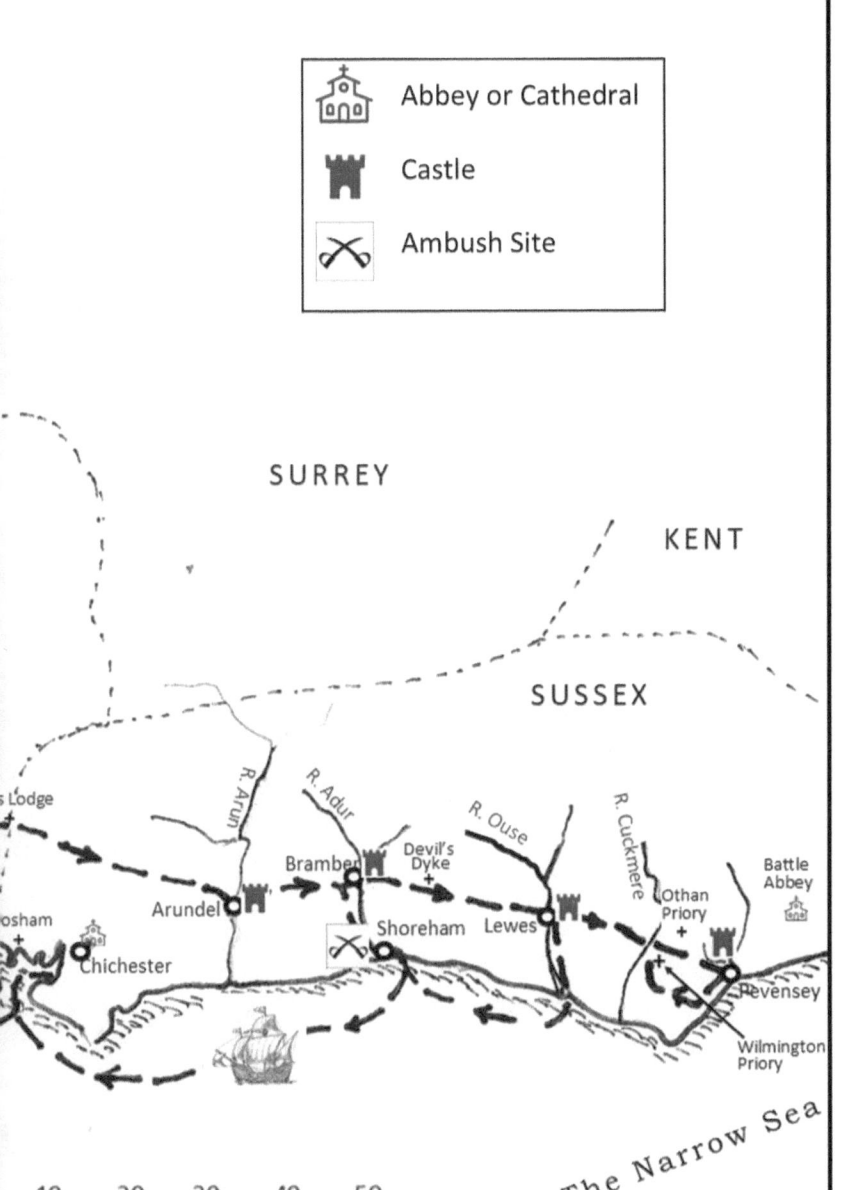

Abbey or Cathedral

Castle

Ambush Site

SURREY

KENT

SUSSEX

s Lodge

R. Arun

R. Adur

R. Ouse

R. Cuckmere

Bramber

Devil's Dyke

Battle Abbey

osham

Arundel

Chichester

Shoreham

Lewes

Othan Priory

Pevensey

Wilmington Priory

The Narrow Sea

10   20   30   40   50

Miles

Chapter 1

The Wettest of Days

The relentless rain swept down the valley towards the river, swollen with an ugly torrent of debris. Huddled in a bothy the man angrily watched the water swirl and suck against the crumbling banks. His pale complexion and deep-set eyes were stretched over high cheek bones pockmarked with scars from recent illness. A thin mouth gave his lower jaw line an intensity of resentment, the nose no more than a bony protuberance giving the whole face a distinct crow like appearance.

A dead sheep tumbled by - torn branches - a dead cat - no end to the destruction of this poor Summer. He thought he would be safe here, but the weather was destroying him. He slammed his fist into the feeble walls of the bothy, causing more harm to the fragile construction. It was destroying the land, too. Erosion of soil had altered the shape of grazing land and whole flocks of sheep were sickening and dying with murrain, no match for this endless greyness. He had hoped to find employment here, but working with wood was what he knew; there were too many flocks here - he needed a place nearer to habitation, if he dared.

He could not stay close to the place where he had killed - he had escaped the hue and cry cunningly, using his wits and his wiry strength, and was now far from home. Indeed, he was now so far from home that it was to his disadvantage not knowing the lie of the land nor where friendly villages might lie. He needed work. Without work he would become a wolfs-head, living rough in some forest – he had not intended that.

He had found this bothy earlier in the day when seeking a place to shelter from the storm. It had once been well constructed, but now it was weather tossed and lacked enough substance to keep him dry. He was too idle to make any repairs however, and lay inside, watching the angry water of the River Yeo rush down towards the distant sea coast. Never an advocate of hard work he now felt too weak to make any effort at improvement. His thin-lipped mouth seemed perpetually compressed in anger, and deep-set cold eyes, the one lazy from birth, were overshadowed with thick, dark eyebrows. He had lost his hat when scrambling over heathland which had left his head unprotected from the vicious rain, so his thick dark hair was plastered to his head giving him a cavernous appearance. The eggs he had stolen earlier were now gone, eaten raw, tossed down his throat carelessly, and he must now eat again.

There were small villages, hamlets up and down this river he knew, but which way to go? Perhaps he had come too far South in his flight. Perhaps he should begin to work his way up river, back into the great deer forest he had skirted some days ago.

He pulled his soaked cloak round his thin shoulders, flexing his muscles against the wet cloth. He was not afraid to steal again if he could find something worth taking, - nor to kill again, if the need arose. He had killed once – he could kill again. He had made a mistake, he knew, in coming so close to this river. It had chilled him and taken him away from what little habitation there was. He needed dry clothes and food. in this pestilent Summer, few folk would willingly give – he would have to take for himself.

As he raised himself from the muddy floor of the bothy he felt a twinge of tooth pain. No, not again. He remembered the piercing pain of a previous tooth agony - he wouldn't go through that again. It rendered him helpless, unable to think clearly and nearly mad from the pain. He chewed on his lip to try to ease the twinge. With squelching boots and hose clinging uncomfortably to him he began his journey Northwards seeking unprotected homes he could rob for dry clothes and victuals. The rain continued to fall in angry, slanting arrows piercing the willow reeds of the now deserted bothy and spitting fiercely into the raging waters of the Yeo.

Matthias Barton and his man Davy splashed wearily over the rising stream bordering the meadow, returning from seeing pupils homeward. Matthias owned the small school for boys of local merchants in Milborne Port, a large village on the borders of Dorset and Somerset. The school was still in its infancy and took place in his own home, becoming more established, now in its second year. Davy normally took the boys as far as the Guildhall in the village, where they were met by family members. Today Matthias had been delivering some carved wooden spoons to a customer of Martin Cooper.

Martin lodged in the barn which was part of Matthias' property, and if the truth be known, Matthias would now like the use of the barn in order to expand the school.

Martin had arrived a year ago, a soldier discharged wounded and therefore unfit for the continuing war with France, destitute, and with a story so full of courage, ill fortune and much suffering that Matthias could not bring himself to raise the question of his leaving. Despite their difference in education and breeding, the two had become friends, unlikely as it seemed, and Martin's life did appear to be gathering momentum now. Out of friendship, Matthias was prepared to be patient. Their horses were wet, rain streamed into their eyes and the wind was rising fast. Davy took note of the loose barn door; that would need repairing before the wind took it.

Two wet Summers in a row seemed dismal. The tracks were mud filled, overflowing ditches under drenched hedgerows making riding with the young scholars unpleasant, and the rain- soaked land did nothing to persuade them that this year's harvest would be any better than last. Bread and vegetables would be precious this year, making people discontented and afraid. There was much talk of unrest further up country.

So far little of this had touched Dorset but Matthias was thankful that his occupation was not connected to the land. He had flourished in his school-mastering and his pupils had increased to such an extent that he was now turning pupils away, which was why he would have liked to have the use of his own barn.

Davy stabled the horses whilst Matthias entered his home, still stung with quickening pleasure and excitement at the thought of Alice waiting for him in the room she had taken so much pleasure in furnishing anew. He liked nothing better than to sit with her in the evenings, talking over the day, watching her face light up and crinkle into laughter at every little snippet of amusement.

Much had changed for him since their marriage six months ago. He had been so afraid that her father would reject him that he had feigned indifference to her, preferring instead to offer her a business arrangement in the school, for she had proved herself to be a worthwhile teacher. Alice, for her part, had found him cold and unbending, lacking emotion and it was not until he had fallen sick with a type of marsh fever after being nearly drowned that she learned of his feelings for her, and his unresolved grief after losing his parents and sisters.

She too had a desire to be cherished once again, for her first husband had deserted his post in the King's army in France to be with a French courtesan leaving her shamed and with a four-year old son. Sir Allard and his courtesan had been subsequently murdered, all of which Matthias knew. Her father, the King's Coroner in Dorset, had attempted to arrange a marriage for her with an older knight, but Alice had rejected the proposition and had begged to be permitted to remain as a widow, working with Matthias as an assistant in his school.

Matthias felt blessed ten-fold when Sir Tobias had expressed his delight at their proposed union, despite Alice being the daughter of a knight and more recently, a Justice of the Peace.

Their wedding feast had been attended by a few close friends - Ezekiel Jacobson, the barber-surgeon and his wife Martha and their two sons who were now numbered among Matthias' pupils, Davy, Matthias' serving man and his wife Elizabeth, Martin Cooper, still lodging in the barn, Lydia and her small daughter Freya and her adopted daughter Ennis. It was an oddly assorted party, but under the circumstances, perfect.

The evening hour was now upon them, and despite the steadily falling rain it was still light enough to enjoy their meal without the use of candles. Matthias, Alice and Luke ate together, a simple plate of buttered chicken with herbs and salad from the garden which Elizabeth took such pride in tending. There were plentiful herbs and leaves to mix together and Elizabeth's manchet loaves served with fresh butter from the village market were always welcomed.

Alice been delighted and excited to organize this room. The oak table round which they sat had been a wedding gift from Sir Tobias and Lady Bridget, and Martin had been commissioned to fashion oak benches to provide seating. Tapestry rugs adorned the walls and the windows were glassed with a thick greenish glass, letting in light and keeping out draught. The floor, uneven flag stones, had simple woollen rugs arranged symmetrically which Elizabeth beat and turned every day. The great fireplace was in use again, Matthias not having used it whilst he was unmarried, logs piled ready for use, and now, even in this wet Summer, Alice and Elizabeth had managed an arrangement of garden flowers and herbs to fill the grate. The bruised leaves and petals gave off a pleasant scent, filling the room with an ambience of which Matthias was proud.

Luke toyed with the food on his trencher, picking carefully among the variety of leaves and turning over the chicken with his spoon. The child was annoying Matthias who took care to hide his irritation. Alice had particularly requested that Luke should eat with them after their marriage rather than be taken away by her maidservant to eat separately. Matthias had readily agreed, understanding that Luke needed to feel part of this new family arrangement, but his reluctance to enjoy his food was beginning to rankle. It caused Alice to watch Luke rather than participate in conversation of late, and Luke was aware of his mother's attention and it appeared to Matthias that he enjoyed this attention. He determined to speak to Alice later to resolve this.

Luke noticed Matthias watching him and laid his spoon down, his efforts at eating finished. Matthias curbed his tongue and remained silent. He felt he was not good at fathering – he had not imagined it would be so difficult. He was doing his best to be a good husband, but he had not reckoned on Luke's antipathy. Whilst Luke was his pupil, there had been no suggestion of trouble but now he was wed to Alice, there was a distinct distance between them. Luke, now six years old, would soon be old enough to graduate to the school in Sherborne where Matthias himself had been schooled and Matthias was anxious that somehow this difficulty between himself and Luke should be resolved before he left the safety of their home and became a boarding pupil with Thomas Copeland.

The repast finished, Luke slipped outside to find Martin Cooper; he enjoyed watching Martin work and Martin was ever content to allow Luke to sit cross legged on the floor in the barn and watch.

He was working on an intricate box for a customer. Since beginning his customised work, Martin had developed a steady stream of work, offering carved pieces rather than trying to compete with other carpenters who had been in the village for longer, some of whom sent work to him if anything more decorative was needed. Luke sat silently, watching as Martin carefully exerted patient carving on the delicate leaves he was fashioning on the front of the box.

Relieved of Luke's presence, Matthias helped himself to an apple from the bowl on the table. He bit into its crisp skin and relished the tart juice of the fruit.

"These came from your father's orchard - his early apples. We could plant some fruit trees, Alice."

"Yes, so we could." Her tone was a little flat, lacking her usual enthusiasm.

"Would you not like our own fruit Alice?" he teased, gently.

"I would like it better if you and Luke were on more friendly terms, Matthias."

"Perhaps he should eat with Lindy instead of sitting with us."

"We agreed that he would feel more comfortable eating with us," Alice demurred.

"Luke is not settled with me," Matthias stated. It was time they faced this difficulty together.

"I do not understand why. We were more settled before we wed - I thought Luke had become fond of you. He still respects you in school, - it is when we are here together that he is difficult." Alice bit her lip as she spoke.

"I have done everything I can to embrace Luke as a son, but it seems he will have none of it. When he is with your father and mother he becomes a natural child again - but here in our own house, he is a different boy - sullen, difficult to converse with, unwilling to engage with me - wanting your attention all the time." Matthias voiced the underlying problem succinctly.

"Are you jealous of him, Matthias?" There was a sudden edge to her voice.

Her suggestion hit him with such force that it was as if he had been physically slapped. She regretted the words almost as she uttered them. The hurt was visible in his eyes, in his sudden clenching of his hands.

He breathed deeply and pushed his bench away from the table.

"Of course I am not, but he will not permit any closeness - it is as if he distrusts me."

"I'm sorry – that was unfair. I had not expected this either."

Matthias paused, tipped her face towards him and looked into her eyes, trying to read her true thoughts. His heart was beating with unspoken fear. How could this be happening to them? He buried his head against her shoulder, found his arms round her waist, pulled her towards him, shaking with the sudden shock of the moment. His arms encircled her waist, feeling her yield to his touch. Desire overcame him as he raised her up and turned her round to face him. She knocked the chair between them away and pressed her body against his, responding to his need. He would have lifted her and carried her to bed had he not seen the child staring balefully at them from the doorway. As Matthias released Alice, Luke turned and ran blindly out into the rain.

Martin was setting out to see Lydia when he saw Luke run out of the house and into the stable. Postponing his journey, he followed the child in.

"Would you like to come with me to see Lydia?" he suggested.

"No thank you," Luke replied, keeping his head averted from Martin. He didn't want anyone to see the easy ears starting in his eyes. Besides, he knew that would mean a slow walk, even for his six- year old legs, adjusting his speed to Martin's crutches and prosthetic limb. He also suspected that Lydia and Martin were fast approaching the awkward state he observed in his mother and Matthias, and how difficult that was; he called Matthias "sir," respectfully enough during the day, but at home it was a different matter. Matthias and his mother would give each other that special look that he had so come to hate, and he had to endure the jibes of his one -time friend in school, Titus, who was older than he and seemed to know more of the ways of the world. Titus had told him that soon the babies would come. That the special look meant babies, that Luke would soon be a nuisance. He tried to avoid Titus now, but it wasn't easy. Titus would whisper to him, "Any babies yet? You can tell - ladies get fatter."

But to Matthias' regret, the babies did not come. Alice thought it was for the best, until Luke had gone to school in Sherborne; every time her courses appeared she was thankful and reassured Matthias that there was nothing wrong - just chance.

Martin sat down on an upturned bucket in the stable.

"Tell me you're not unhappy for your mother, lad."

Luke blushed and scuffed the ground with the toe of his boot.

"It's alright, Martin. I just want everything to be as it was when we were living with Grandfather and Grandmother."

"You have to go forward, Luke. You cannot travel backwards. Don't make the mistake of making your mother doubt herself."

Luke frowned. He didn't truly understand what Martin was talking about.

"Are you sure you don't want to come with me to Lydia's?"

"Quite sure, Martin."

Martin sat with Lydia in her simple cottage, so much improved since she had first lived here, thanks to Martin's many repairs and alterations. A fine wooden table with four stout chairs graced the front of the room, and a cupboard for her few crocks stood in one corner. Martin had made a shelf with wooden hooks for outdoor cloaks, and the floor was now covered with fresh rushes daily. The door latches were now secure and the children had cots made by Martin, who had fashioned a simple ladder to their one upstairs room where Freya and Ennis slept. Some of the wood he used was wood left over from commissions he had completed, but he had never taken this as his due, only with permission or in some cases, payment to the owners. His gratitude for her friendship knew no bounds and he had worked tirelessly for her whenever he could, building and improving her furniture. Sometimes Lydia slept upstairs in the same room as the girls and at other times, as her whim took her, she used a palette in her front room. The back room served as a kitchen, with wood fire and access to the outdoor privy, shared with neighbours.

Martin was always happy to sit with her of an evening. Her acceptance of his disability and her uncomplicated lifestyle gave him a sense of peace. She asked nothing from him; what he gave, he gave willingly and she accepted with grace. Matthias had once told him that it was wrong to think that he could never be more than a friend to her, but he had never quite dared to test this. If he was rejected, how could he come and sit with her again in this atmosphere of stillness and friendship?

This evening they spoke of Luke. Lydia had adopted Ennis, fleeing from an abusive man who had killed her mother and had made a success of the child. She was clean, polite, was learning household tasks, and sometimes Martin taught her letters, for Martin had some education. Lydia had just laughed when Martin offered to teach her to read, and Martin had observed that Lydia was right – she did not have the appetite for learning, but Ennis did, and Martin often played simple number and letter games with the child.

"You think Luke is missing having Lady Alice to himself?" Lydia asked.

"It is likely," Martin answered, watching Lydia smooth Freya's hair as she prepared her daughter for bed. Lydia was dressed in a simple blue tunic, belted at her slim waist, a light veil covering her hair. The very simplicity of her caught at Martin's throat and he wondered if he dared offer her more than his friendship.

"He cannot accept the new relationship. I think it embarrasses him to see Matthias affectionate with his mother. He has no memory of Sir Allard at all, and he knew Matthias as his schoolmaster first before anything else. It is difficult to know how to help. Matthias tries very hard to curb his obvious affection when Luke is nearby, but how hard that must be - he's not used to suddenly being wedded and a father all at once."

Lydia frowned down at the toddler on her knee, thinking of solutions but finding none.

"It was easy for me to take Ennis," she said slowly, thinking it through, "There was no man here, and if there had been I don't think she would have stayed. She had learned only fear and beatings from her mother and the man. She settled quickly and you were not able to come here for quite some time due to your injuries. I visited you – you were not here as a rival."

Sometimes Martin was surprised by Lydia's clear thinking. He reached out and touched her hand, suddenly moved to ask her what he had not dared for so many months:

"Lydia, how would it be if there were a man here once more?"

Lydia was not swift to answer, and Martin felt the hot blood rush into his face as his heart dropped. She looked at him curiously and seemed to shrink into her own thoughts for several moments, leaving Martin suspended in time. In truth, Lydia was remembering Ben, her first husband, murdered days before Freya was born. Freya was now two Summers old and Lydia held Ben's memory still in her heart, but Martin had grown on her, his kindness, his courage, his affection for both the children, his attempts at bringing some laughter and warmth back into her simple life. She met his eyes shyly and placed her hands on his own.

"We could try, Martin. I still think of Ben and how he would have loved watching Freya grow, but sometimes when I think of Ben, his image escapes me and yours creeps in. Every time you say you need to leave Master Barton's barn and find somewhere of your own, my heart lurches because I would miss you. That must mean I feel comfortable with you."

"I am not much of a catch, Lydia," he commented, wryly. "I am nearly blind in one eye and seriously lame, in spite of all Master Jacobson has done for me, but I love coming here, and I look forward to seeing you every day. I believe that's pretty close to loving you. We'll be hand-fast at the church door as soon as I can arrange matters with Matthias."

"There is still that difference between us," Lydia faltered, suddenly aware of her place in the village.

"What difference?"

"You call Master Barton by his Christian name...I still call him Master Barton and am a little nervous when I see him. You can read and write...I am unlettered, and as you saw, I am not quick to learn such things. How will we be together when there is this difference?"

"You forget, I once called him Master Barton...but I have lived there for two years and seen many sides of him. I have worked for him in the school room and been tended by him... he does not stand on ceremony. I value his friendship, but I still understand my place in the world. I understand the difference between us and we both respect that difference. My education, poor though it is, is due to Sir Allard, who taught me so that I could become his squire in battle. I have been fortunate in that...less fortunate in other ways. Lydia, believe me, my fortunes began again when you moved my fallen crutch towards me with your foot, and then offered me bread. That is our story."

Rain had followed him all the way as he moved further North, leaving the cursed River Yeo behind him. A stolen mule took him to the edge of the great deer forest he had noticed during his flight South. He had ridden uncomfortably, with no saddle or reins and was glad to abandon the beast before finding shelter amongst the trees. He must be wary; he would prefer to reach a village or town, dry out and seek work. He did not wish to meet up with bands of wolfheads, men who were outside the law. He knew he was indeed outside the law in reality, but he had reached a place where he was not known and was out of the reach of his fellow citizens. He needed a town in which he could seek work.

He skirted the deer forest the next day and joined a track. Which way would benefit him best?

A carter on the way gave him information. East – Shaftesbury with a great nunnery and markets or West towards

Sherborne and Exeter. Sherborne Abbey was rebuilding, so he was told, so he opted for Sherborne, and hopped up behind the carter.

The track was water logged in places, muddy and difficult to negotiate, but today the rain had at least ceased, and the sun, when it came through, still had a little Summer strength so he was able to dry out to a certain extent.

The carter was a Sherborne man, returning from delivering hides to nearby Henstridge. He was happy to talk about his home town and soon it became clear that there might well be work to be found in the Abbey or the Almshouses where there was building going on. The carter chattered on, oblivious to the lack of response. He spoke of the fire in the Abbey, of the building work, of the collection of money made by the townspeople for the Almshouse, of the bad feeling between the Abbey and the town – by the time the carter arrived at his destination in Newbridge, the man knew enough about Sherborne to feel confident that he would find employment here.

Sherborne in the early evening was rain washed cobbles, glistening eaves, mellow stone buildings dripping with excess rainwater and behind it all, the magnificent backdrop of the Abbey, marred now with scaffolding and scorched stone work, but never the less, awe-inspiring in its serenity. Behind this façade were packed tenement buildings, ale houses of uncertain quality, narrow streets with leats full of dirty water which carried away night soil and heavy rains often spilled over making the walkways unpleasantly wet. He had walked from Newbridge, at the Eastern end of the town and now stood at the top of Cheap Street, looking down the hill towards the great Abbey. There were shops, closing up at this time, drawing in their awnings and signs, two wealthy looking inns – not for him until he had dried out properly – the usual collection of street urchins playing in the mud, and various merchants supervising their apprentices as trading ceased for the day. On the right-hand side as he walked down he noticed several tall hall houses, very well set up. He studied these carefully. It would be these he could target for clothes and food – silver plate, too, he wouldn't mind guessing. He paused as if adjusting his boots, the better to notice side doors, loose roof tiles, faulty window catches. Yes, he would return here after dark and find himself some dry clothes, food and something worth selling to give himself some coin before seeking work.

Chapter 2

Mishaps Around the Misericords

Sherborne was dry for a change, with the sun still offering some heat. The mood was cheerful as the labourers toiled in the Abbey, for their foreman was a merry soul who believed that a cheerful workforce made for a blessed result. He had taken on a selection of day labourers to try and catch up on time lost through poor weather, for some of the work was still outside, and the wet Summer had put them behind, much to Abbot Bradford's displeasure.

The chinking of the chisels as the stones were shaped echoed through the cavernous Abbey, fine dust dancing in the air, choking the lungs of the watching monks. Further in, the master carver, clear of the dust, knelt on the hard stones as he fashioned delicate wood carvings beneath the monks' choir stalls. He had lived and worked in Sherborne all his life and knew intricately the personalities of the place. As he worked on the fruit held by his depiction of a market stall holder, he wondered mischievously whether he dared use the old schoolmaster as a model. It would be quite a joke to see Thomas Copeland beating a boy, carved for ever under the choir stalls. He might try that next, when he had completed this one. He was a careful, skilled worker, one for whom the poor Summer had had little effect. He watched as his young apprentice gathered up the shavings from the floor and dusted the face of the fruit carefully.

The man watching him waited for a suitable break in the work before coughing carefully to attract attention.

Edric, master carver, turned irritably, disliking the interruption. He was mature in years, and his eyes troubled him as he worked. He could not afford to make mistakes, so his concentration was stretched to the limit.

"Well?"

"I am seeking a position working with wood, Master."

"There is no work here. I have enough skilled men. Try the almshouse." Edric turned back to his work, squinting at the completed fruit with satisfaction, the enquiry already forgotten. The rough face of the market trader grasping his basket of fruit glowed with the sheen of the polished wood. Edric had done well...there were more to complete, but this one was fine enough, - just one more polish. He ran his hand over the smooth wood, caressing the rounded feel.

The hot anger of the rejected man rose in his throat; he glanced at the young apprentice who smiled tentatively at him, but the smile was misinterpreted. Rage at being mocked made him blind. He lunged forward, knocking the youth to the stone floor with such violence that his head split immediately, blood staining the stone floor under the choir stalls where they were working.

Edric shouted, and the man was gone, fleeing up the aisle, out of the door, jumping over loose stones lying in his way and Edric's cry for help was met by labourers who were unaware of the violence in their efforts to stem the flow of blood and assist in helping the young apprentice.

The lad sat propped against a choir stall, head swathed in cloth hurriedly brought from the monk's infirmary, Brother Francis summoned to tend him. His white face made the blood seem even more vivid, staining the cloths with which he was padded.

One of the younger, more agile apprentices working further up the aisle dropped his tools and shouting "harrow!" chased after the fleeing man, others joining the chase.

Although unfamiliar with the tracks and alleys in this town, the man was adept at flight and concealment. He was soon flat beneath a discarded cart behind a row of tenements, shabby and dilapidated. The hunt for him, begun too late, was over.

Matthias was delighted to hear Martin's news; he had long thought Lydia would accept his offer and had on several occasions encouraged Martin to think on the possibility. His pleasure was the greater because it afforded himself and Alice the opportunity to use the barn to expand the school. He would never have turned Martin out, but the chance had presented itself, and he and Alice were now talking over the possibilities. Alice was also planning a wedding feast for Martin and Lydia, to be held in the barn itself. She was excited to be able to plan the day for them and was already seeking local fiddlers for dancing.

"Do you think that's a step too far?" Matthias suggested, pleased by the sight of her flushed, excited face as she listed her ideas for the feast, their spats over Luke forgotten for the moment.

"Why?"

"Martin is unable to dance....it wouldn't do to make him feel uncomfortable on his wedding night"

Her face fell.

"I hadn't considered that. I only thought it would make such a lively air to the festivities."

"Who would you invite?"

"For Martin and Lydia, it would be people from the village...their neighbours...maybe some of Martin's clients... some of the boys from school might be asked. It would give him a boost in the village. He has lived quite a protected life with you here. It's time he embraced the village more."

Matthias considered. He saw that Alice had thought carefully about Martin's place in the community, and he loved her for that. He was fond of Martin; he had become an unlikely friend and Matthias was delighted that Martin had finally believed in himself sufficiently to take this step.

"Ezekiel and his family will come...and your parents...it will be quite an evening."

Sir Tobias was perplexed by a recent series of robberies in Sherborne. The bailiff had called on him to inform him of the attack in the Abbey and mentioned the sudden prolific robberies in the town. There were always pick pockets and foists in the area, especially on market days; Sherborne was no different to any other place, but these house robberies were silent, persistent and cunning. No trace could be found of a point of entry, and there appeared to be no damage done to property. Good silver had been lifted, items of clothing, food and whenever possible, coin, if it had been left unguarded. In one case, a gentleman's purse was stolen from the very room in which he slept.

"These robberies have been committed on several recurring nights?" queried the Coroner.

The bailiff nodded, scratching his beard as he spoke. They were in the Coroner's usual room at the George Inn, no fire in the grate as it was still Summer, despite the now shortening days.

"Tell me more about this attack in the Abbey."

"Apparently the man who attacked had been refused work by the Master carver...he lunged at the apprentice with his dagger. The lad is making a recovery, but he will be scarred... he thought he had smiled sympathetically at the man."

"Do we have a description? Was there no chase?"

"The description is vague. Edric, the carver, did not look up from his work, and the lad can only say he was of middle height, dressed as a workman in sombre clothing...he thought he had a dark beard but he cannot be sure. The chase was slow to take off – the man was fast. By the time the cry had gone up he was out of the Abbey door and running hard."

"A fit man, then, to be sure."

"Aye, fleet of foot and alert...went to ground quite easily. Maybe used to hiding himself."

The Coroner grunted. He had no real hope of finding the culprit, but he had his scribe write a description, such as it was.

Now he had been appointed Justice of the Peace as well as Coroner, his work had increased, and he relied on local bailiffs and reeves to keep him well informed. He had a good relationship with this bailiff; he wished it was so in every place. Some were mildly dishonest; others were through and through corrupt. Honesty in high places was hard to find, especially as the unrest in the country was spreading from the top. The young King was too easily influenced by the power-seeking men around him, too keen on his prayers and philosophies. Leadership was not his best attribute. The Coroner was afraid for the state of the country when he learned of great lords arguing amongst themselves, making decisions which seemed against the common good and seizing power which was not rightfully theirs.

There was unrest at court in Windsor also, as Sir Tobias had discovered in an uncomfortable day spent waiting in the forecourts with other such knights as himself summoned from the shires to receive their new status, surrounded by courtiers who were angling for positions in the service of the young king, dressed in their preposterous samite and silk garments, cut to reveal every line of their young fit bodies and much more besides. Sir Tobias felt uncomfortable with the sights. Worse still were the primped ladies, elaborate head dresses, low cut bodices revealing creamy white flesh.

Sir Tobias had been there to receive his seal of office as a newly appointed Justice of the Peace and emerged dismayed by unseemly wrangling between Duke Humphrey and the Royal Council. The atmosphere had at times been poisonous, venom emanating between courtiers who supported one faction or the other. Many of them, too, were clothed in extravagant robes, bejewelled, well-oiled in face and hair, perfumed and pampered. There were clear shenanigans between the gorgeously attired ladies of the court and the young men, and obvious unrest on the streets outside.

Many of the courtiers spent their days hunting in the lush green forests around Windsor, hanging around the sumptuous rooms where they might catch the eye of the young king or his advisors or making love with court ladies, oblivious of their marital status.

Outside the castle the poor were no different from the poor in Sherborne, Sir Tobias noted - there were simply more of them. The streets were grubby, houses nearly meeting in the middle of the street with windows overhanging. The leat down the centre of each street carried unsavoury night soil, offal and other detritus. The great gates of the town were shut fast at curfew and traders were tightly constrained. He was relieved to be able to leave and return to Sherborne and the quiet peace of his home in Purse Caundle.

The uneasy experience stayed with him, however. He had been aware, in his short time at Court, of the talk of finding a suitable bride for the young king, who was now sixteen, and able to rule in his own right. He had seen the King from afar, - looking younger than his years, with a weak chin, pale eyes and pallid complexion. He was flanked by advisors, including Duke Humphrey and his uncle Cardinal Beaufort. Sir Tobias, at the back of the crowd, had bowed his knee and when he looked up, the King had left.

Sir Tobias sighed heavily; he had seen battle in France in his lifetime; he did not wish to experience civil war as well. Matters of state seemed too precarious under this young king. The country needed a leader. He was careful not to voice his fears; he had no wish to be accused of treachery, but in his wisdom, he was becoming concerned.

Collecting his scribe as he left, the two men walked down Cheap Street towards the Abbey, leading their horses. Thomas Cope was talking to a neighbour in the street, and as he passed, Sir Tobias made mention of Luke's possible starting date in the school.

"How old is Luke now?" Thomas asked, pleased to have retained Sir Tobias as a client.

"He is six years old...he will be seven next Maytime. Will you have space for him?"

"I will indeed," Thomas replied. "He is fortunate in having Matthias Barton as father now."

"We are delighted at their union," Sir Tobias replied, pleased to have been able to firm Luke's place.

He mused further as he followed his scribe down towards the Abbey. He had not been inside for some time, anxious to avoid Abbot Bradford's caustic nature, but he wondered as he led his horse through the busy market how the building work was progressing.

"Wait a little, Stephen," he muttered, as the rough scaffolding around the Abbey came into view.

"Hold the horses a moment. I have a mind to see what progress is made, and we can see how the Almshouse is progressing, too."

He made his way carefully through the side entrance, picking his way over hewn stones and greeting the workmen as he went. Most of them were local men who were familiar with the Coroner. He looked up to where the great bell tower had been. It had fallen disastrously during the worst of the fire, crashing to the ground whilst the monks could only watch helplessly. Work seemed slow to progress. Abbot Bradford was grimly determined to make the townspeople pay for the damage caused, and silver was slow in coming, but frequent collections and raised taxes were gradually making a difference.

He spied one of the brothers, robe caught up discreetly round his knees to avoid the thick dust made by the breaking of the stones and nodded to him. He was calculating with the foreman on a piece of slate, frowning as they measured the stones needed for the next piece of wall.

Sir Tobias moved into the central aisle, largely untouched by the fire, although stained a little by the ferrous nature of the stones under such extreme heat. He wondered idly as he passed whether the stain would fade in time. He found the Master carver Edric still at work and watched for a few moments as he knocked his chisel carefully into the wood, intent on his work. Edric paused to sharpen his tool and saw the Coroner watching. He touched his woollen cap respectfully.

"I'm still without my lad, Sir Coroner. No sign of his attacker?"

"Gone to ground, I'm afraid," replied Sir Tobias. "We will continue to search, but the hue and cry was slow to realise there had been an attack, it appeared."

Edric grunted, wiping his sharpened chisel on his overall.

"We were working peacefully out of sight of the main body of men," he explained. "It took several moments for them to understand that there had been a villainous attack. My lad was bleeding heavily. He'll recover, but he needs to be fit enough to stand with me all day."

The Coroner moved on, knelt in prayer for a few moments in the Lady Chapel to remember Ben and to thank God for the path that had led Matthias to find peace with his beloved daughter and grandson.

Unbeknown to the Coroner, Luke was at this moment considering flight. He was very confused, for sitting at this moment on a hard bench in the schoolroom, he was listening to Matthias as his schoolmaster and drinking in the story which Matthias was sharing, Alexander the Great, the best story he had heard - a hero. He had always loved the way Matthias brought stories like this to life. At the same time, he glowered as he recalled the gentle murmur of voices from behind the closed bed chamber that morning, his mother's soft laugh, Matthias' deeper voice and then a silence, during which Luke could not imagine what they were doing. He felt neglected; before the marriage of his mother to Matthias, he had been able to nestle up to her, warm and smelling of sleepy love for him. Now he had a little bed of his own in an adjoining room, made by Matthias as a place which he could call his own, Matthias had said. He didn't want a place to call his own. His place was by his mother's side.

He looked up as his name was called. Now he felt stupid; he couldn't answer the question asked of him because his mind had been elsewhere.

Titus had teased him again that very morning about babies...he heard Titus snigger as he was unable to answer Matthias' question to him.

"You need to listen harder, Luke," Matthias told him, surprise in his voice, for Luke was normally attentive in school, in spite of the difficulties at home.

The boys always had a break for a slight repast of whatever they had brought from home half way through their day, and Luke took the opportunity to move away from the other boys who were kicking an old inflated pig's bladder around. He moved stealthily beyond Martin's barn and out through the trees on the other side. No-one saw him go and the afternoon wore on, Alice believing him to have been retained with Matthias and the older boys and Matthias believing him to be in the curtained room for the younger boys with Alice.

Davy gathered up the scholars for their ride home, and glanced round at the two Jacobson boys, who waited always for Ezekiel to collect them.

"Where is Luke today?" he asked, a little puzzled, as Luke normally waited with them, often playing a game with them whilst waiting for Ezekiel.

"I haven't seen him this afternoon," replied Thomas, the older of the two.

"He wasn't with us either," volunteered Daniel, as Davy prepared to move off with the four scholars who would be met in the centre of the village.

Davy wheeled his horse round to call through the open school room door to Matthias.

"Master...have you seen Luke? I think he is not with us."

Matthias paused in his work and came to the door. He shaded his eyes against the lowering sun. He could see no sign of Luke. Alice came through from her curtained small room, wiping her hands on a cloth.

"Luke has been with you all day today Matthias."

"No, Alice...he was with me this morning. I thought he was with you this afternoon."

"I did not think to query it" Alice faltered, "Where is he then?"

"Is he with Martin?"

He was not, and Martin came from the barn, concern knitting his brow as he remembered Luke's recent obvious unhappiness.

Davy cantered off with the scholars, shouting that he would ask in the village and return home at once to search.

Alice and Matthias divided their land between them and trudged over the meadow, walked the adjoining tracks, ran down to the stream which followed the bottom of the valley and called Luke's name repeatedly. There was no sign of him.

Distractedly, Alice returned to the house, passing her hand over her hot face. Her wimple was dislodged, hair tumbling round her shoulders unrestrained by the head-dress. Martin was waiting with Elizabeth, Davy's wife, as she returned.

"Lady Alice, have you considered that Luke may have tried to walk to your father's house?" Martin suggested. Alice sank down on the wall by the herb garden and plucked a piece of lavender, crushing it fiercely between her fingers.

"Of course, I had not thought of that, but why would he run out of school? Who has upset him so?"

"I think he is finding it difficult to settle to new arrangements," Martin tentatively began.

Lady Alice looked at him sharply; Martin felt he had overstepped the mark.

"Forgive me." he began, hesitantly.

"No, it's alright, Martin. He has been eating and sleeping poorly, perhaps I should allow him to eat alone after his lessons have finished."

Matthias felt there was some value in riding out towards Sir Tobias' home and saddled the mare to ride out to Purse Caundle. The land by the stream was muddy due to so much rain this Summer, and his hose was caked with mud, but there was some urgency as the days were shortening, and Luke would have little idea of how to shelter from the night. Besides, there were reports of robberies in the area, which meant gangs of lawless men might be operating in these outlying villages.

"This is so unlike Luke...he is such a home loving boy. I thought he would flourish here with us..."

Matthias found himself stumbling over his words as he mounted, frantically going over in his mind what he had said to Luke in the schoolroom - nothing more than he would have said to any scholar who clearly had not been paying attention - what else had happened lately? Nothing of note - he, Matthias, had tried to be circumspect regarding his open love and affection towards Lady Alice, aware that Luke was uncomfortable with displays of emotion. Strange, he had been so delighted when their forthcoming marriage had been planned, and at first had seemed to enjoy his new life. Where and when had this all gone so wrong?

He was halfway to Purse Caundle, musing over anything he had said to Luke that might have been misunderstood, when he noticed a carter coming towards him. The axles of the cart were grinding slowly through the muddy track, making heavy work of the journey. Ale casks on the back of the open cart were lashed securely; as Matthias reined his horse in to the side to give the carter room to pass he recognized the man as a near neighbour of Lydia, a stunted little man whose cart was his pride and joy and who made a meagre living by fetching and carrying goods for other traders.

He drew level with Matthias and touched his forelock respectfully, knowing Matthias by sight.

He pushed back his hood and rested his reins.

"Master, I've a cargo for you I believe." He clambered awkwardly down from his rough seat, throwing the reins over the nag's scrawny back. Walking with difficulty through the thick mud oozing in the side ruts of the track, he leaned into the back of the conveyance and grasped the arm of the boy lying in the back, between two ale casks.

He gripped Luke's body securely as he lifted him out of the back and put him down in the driest part of the lane.

"I did reckon young master shouldn't be on the track alone - he was making heavy work of the mud and there's more rain to come."

For a brief moment Matthias was bereft of speech, willing himself not to say the wrong thing to Luke, who was shivering now with apprehension and shock. He couldn't believe that he had dared to wander so far alone; he was afraid that Matthias would be angry in front of this rough man who had plucked him out of the ditch when the cart lumbered up to him. The man smelled of stale sweat, onions, ale - but he had not been unkind. He had just picked him up and dumped him in the back of the cart between two of the lashed ale casks and told him he would take him home. Luke was so tired and dirty that he had not argued. He had cried a little in the privacy of his place between the ale casks, but now he was standing on the track waiting for Matthias to speak.

"Come up in front of me and hold on to the saddle horn," Matthias told Luke, gruffly. The carter lifted Luke onto the mare, Matthias adjusted his position in the saddle to give Luke some room, Luke's cold hands gripped the leather saddle horn. Matthias fumbled in his purse for a silver piece for the carter.

"Thankee Sir. I'm sure t'was an adventure which went wrong."

As Matthias turned his horse round in the lane, he somehow doubted the truth of that.

Martin told Lydia the next day how subdued the incident had made Matthias and Lady Alice.

He sensed the relief which washed over Lady Alice as Matthias rode into the gate, Luke perched uncomfortably in front of him. Matthias was reminded of the difference between the journey he had once made with Ennis in front of him. She had leant back into the warmth of his body, cradled in his cloak, shivering with fear but taking comfort from his proximity. Luke, his stepson, kept himself as upright as he was able, silent, his six-year old self wrapped tightly, tensely into himself.

Alice had uttered a small scream of relief before Luke tumbled himself down into her outstretched arms. She had carried him into the house, away from prying eyes, and Matthias was left to dismount, leading his horse into the stable where Davy took the reins from him. Martin had watched sadly as he noticed Matthias hesitate slightly before following Lady Alice into the house, closing the door behind him. He observed that Davy deliberately spent longer than usual grooming and feeding the animals, anxious to afford the family privacy.

"This was not good, Martin, was it?"

"No Lydia. Luke was in school today as usual, but he had his meals with the maid. There may have been privacy, but I don't think there has been much healing."

"But what is there to heal?" Lydia asked, perplexed.

"I don't rightly understand, my love." Freya nestled against Martin's leg, pulling herself upright and laying her head against his knee. Martin ruffled her hair with his hand, squinting down with his one good eye. "Maybe I should talk to Luke about his father."

Martin had been squire to Sir Allard in France before being mortally wounded. Sir Allard had deserted his post as Captain and had subsequently been murdered with Celeste, his leman; Martin had struggled home to tell Lady Alice of her husband's decision to leave with Celeste, enduring pain and hardship to reach England and fulfil what he believed his captain had wished him to do.

"What would you tell him? That his father deserted his mother and left with another woman...worse...a French woman....no, that would not do at all, Martin."

"I had rather thought to explain how I first knew his father and what fun he could be...how his mother would miss that companionship...would that not do, Lydia?"

"Better, but might it not be better still to wait and see if Luke is interested in the kind of man his real father was?"

Martin dropped a kiss on Freya's head and prepared to leave, picking up his crutches and adjusting his new leg for the journey home.

"You are probably right, Lydia. You are so lucky in Ennis – she has fitted well into your little family."

Martin considered on his slow way home how both families had problematic backgrounds to explain to their children as they grew. Luke was the son of a lesser knight who had fought in the dying French wars with honour until he had met Celeste. Luke's paternal grandfather was also a knight but one who had chosen to ignore his grandson once Lady Alice's father had petitioned for the return of the marriage dowry. Luke's mother was the daughter of the Coroner and a Justice of the Peace, also a knight. Alice was their only child and Luke their only grandchild. From Martin's humble beginnings he had considered Lady Alice, lovely though she was, to be rather spoiled although she had proved to be a hard worker and a gifted teacher. Luke for all his six years had been the constant companion of his mother and the darling of his grandsire and grandame. He was unused to sharing his position with anybody else. Matthias, now his stepfather, had lost all his family at a young age, had made his own salvation through travel and work, and had fallen in love with this beguiling widow, aware of her circumstances and family. His own father had risen high in the estimation of royal circles and had been a well-respected landowner, leaving Matthias with a fine house, a little land but no family and a desperate longing for love and family once more.

Martin had no family to speak of…his mother had run off with a tinker, he knew of no other family. He had met Lydia when he was begging; Lydia had offered him bread when he was at his lowest point, as was she, having lost her husband to murder. Freya had been born just after her father's body had been found and Lydia was still mourning him when she first offered the half blind and lame Martin her bread. Ennis joined Lydia's family after her mother had been burnt to death by a lover from whom Ennis had fled in her night shift, being found by Matthias and brought to the safety of Lydia's home. Martin had formed a friendship with Lydia which had grown into love, but the back story of their children was as problematic as that of Matthias and Alice, each in its different way.

As he nursed his aching tooth, the man felt himself lucky that Sherborne was small, - so small that there were no walls surrounding it, no gates which would be closed and guarded as night fell, no moated entrance. He was able to come and go at will, unhindered by stone, lock or water. The only troublesome water was the unending rain which had started again. Was there ever such a dismal Summer as this one, now drawing to a miserable close. Crops were failing, beasts falling ill, - Winter would be hard. He had clothed himself thanks to his clever thieving on the journey, and now his thieving was directed at silver, anything which could be converted to coin. The trouble was, he did not dare try to convert it here in Sherborne for fear of being recognized in such a small place.

He had found himself a derelict dwelling on the edge of Ackerman Street where he had made a sleeping place of sorts for himself, a place to store his ill- gotten goods before he could decide how to sell them and a roof under which to crouch in the dark, planning his next move.

Hitting out at the young apprentice in the Abbey had been stupid; he recognized that. The red mist had descended on him when he saw the lad smirk at the refusal of the Master carver. He wished he could undo that, - not because he was sorry he had injured the youth but because it was preventing him now from asking for work at the almshouse in case he was recognized. He considered how he could alter his appearance. His hair had grown longer and become tangled. If he could obtain a means of cutting it he could shear it short. Stubble had grown unchecked on his chin...perhaps he should walk to the nearest village and seek out a barber to shave him...he had sufficient coin for that. Maybe he could even sell one or two pieces in a different location.

His decision made, he settled down on his rough pile of coverings and closed his eyes.

Several days later Edric was ready to start on his next carving. First, he needed to sketch it out roughly, measuring the space available for the detail he planned to include. This carving would fit under the monk's choir stall like the previous one. He planned it as a wife beating a truculent husband, the energy and enjoyment of her task reflected in her face as the fellow bent over to receive the blows. He grinned to himself as he wielded the charcoal stick, giving her rounded cheeks and plump, capable arms. The husband was smaller, thinner, weedier as he bent to her stick. He screwed up his eyes to view his sketch.

The distant sounds from the masons and their labourers were regular, steady. Soon the day labourers would need to be released to bring in the harvest although it would be a poor harvest this year. After that, the days would grow shorter and the work might cease until the Winter was over and done with. He missed his apprentice sorely. The lad was still suffering from strange blackouts, fainting fits. Until these passed he could not work again.

A man stood at his shoulder watching him sketch. He studied it intently with his deep-set eyes, noticing the places where the wood needed to be gouged more deeply to give substance to the face, admiring the muscular lines of the arms of the angry wife. He ached to take up a tool and begin to carve but he did not dare. Instead he meekly admired the work, making Edric aware of his presence.

The Master carver turned to study his visitor. It was good to hear another voice, especially one admiring the work. Every workman loves to be praised and Edric was no different.

"Do you always work alone, Master?"

"My apprentice is indisposed...he will return when he is well."

"Would you accept help from a fellow such as myself until he is well?"

"What do you know about wood? Where have you come from?"

Edric laid down his charcoal and studied the man facing him. Sombre wool tunic over dark green hose roughly pushed into boots...no weapon that he could see...tunic belted with a plain leather strip...buckle without embellishment....light sleeveless jerkin over the tunic.....looked a plain sort of fellow. His hair was cut short, topped by a woollen cap worn slightly to one side. Edric could see no harm in giving him work if he was willing to do the simple tasks of an apprentice.

"Are you content to perform menial tasks while I work?"

"Indeed I am. That's a good piece of oak you have ready there."

"All this work will be done in oak. Start tomorrow at daybreak."

Edric turned back to his work, leaving the man grinning slyly to himself. He had work with wood! That was a start... he had been forced to leave his tools behind when he had fled his home...if he was careful he could acquire some basic tools here and then move on. He had taken a risk, approaching the very man he'd approached previously, but he'd taken care to change his appearance, alter his voice and general demeanour; he also knew that returning to the scene of crime and asking for work was something few people would imagine. Often one could hide in the most open of fashions.

Chapter 3

Spare the Rod.......

Alice was watching Elizabeth brew their ale. It was something always done by the serving people in her father's house, and even when married to Allard, Alice had had no reason to be involved. Now she set herself to learn these household tasks, even though Elizabeth cooked and brewed for them all. The ale was brewed every few days from barley, just enough to service Matthias and his household.

"We are lucky to have our own well," Elizabeth observed, as she measured out water for the ale brew. "There are some places where water is not so plentiful, and that causes problems for the brewing. Not only do we have our own, but it is clear and sweet, which helps the flavour of the ale."

"Will there be enough grain to see us through the Winter?" Alice wondered. She had never had to consider this when living in her father's household, and although Matthias was not without means, Alice had become aware of differences in the way the household operated.

"Davy thinks the harvest will be poor this year. They are ready for the men to cut, but the grains will not be plump and fulsome. We will have to choose our grain carefully from market, if there is any available. It has been too wet this Summer."

The Coroner's household was run by their steward who organized the serving folk efficiently; Alice had no reason to stray into the kitchen, buttery or scullery to see how they worked. Now she was in a household which was significantly smaller and less regulated. Matthias had lived as a bachelor, retaining Davy and Elizabeth as his manservant and cook, needing little else when he came home from the continent. Alice saw no reason to change things at present and was enjoying learning these simple tasks from Elizabeth. They had no need of a steward or multiple servants.

Alice watched as Elizabeth, sleeves rolled up, began to mash the grain, pounding hard with the wort stick. The grain had previously been left to ferment and was now ready to mash with water.

"Why do you always use the same stick?" Alice had noticed that Elizabeth had used a stick from a corner of the brewing table which seemed dirty.

"We need the wort from the last batch, Mistress. It helps to ferment the brew. It's not dirt - it's matter from the previous brew." Elizabeth continued to pound, breathing heavily. Alice felt guilty watching without helping, but was afraid she would hinder in her ignorance.

She glanced towards the door; she could hear distantly Matthias' voice chanting in Latin for the scholars, Luke among them this morning. What on earth had possessed him to run off? Her attention had wandered from Elizabeth's task.

She had dressed carefully for this lesson from Elizabeth, not wanting to be seen as a burden needing to protect fine clothes. In truth, her new life as Matthias' wife was still exciting and new, but she could not help but notice the differences between life here and life in her father's home - even in her late husband's home. In both those places she had been pampered to a certain extent, indulged to allow leisure to occupy most of her day. She had played with Luke, ridden out with him, visited the stables to play with puppies, kittens, and in her late husband's home there had been hawks to handle, hunting parties to entertain. The sombre experience of Allard's betrayal of her and her strengthening affection for Matthias had changed her, yet she was still learning to embrace his lifestyle. That she loved him was not in doubt;

she thrilled to his touch, loved to enfold herself in his arms as they bedded, was breathless with pleasure at his lovemaking and rarely refused his advances. She knew that he yearned for her to quicken with child, but she was always relieved when every month her courses appeared. She hardly understood why this should be so; she had been delighted when Luke was born so quickly after her union with Allard. Was her body somehow trying to protect Luke until he was more settled? She had not expected Luke to behave in this way. It hurt her to see Matthias unhappy with Luke's behaviour, and she didn't understand it, either.

"The mixture now needs to rest, Mistress."

Alice shook herself back into the present.

"Thank you, Elizabeth"

Her next lesson would be bread making. She was determined to understand the work required to run a household such as this, even though Elizabeth was competent and content to do everything needed.

Alice returned to the schoolroom, leaving Elizabeth in the kitchen with Davy. She was planning to give some extra help to Ezekiel's youngest son, who was lagging behind in his letters. She prepared a copying slate for him and settled down for the afternoon.

Luke and Titus were working together on learning by heart a Latin text Matthias had set. Luke had tried hard to set himself apart from Titus, but Matthias misunderstood his pleading eyes and coupled them together for the exercise.

Luke repeated the words aloud several times, hoping that Titus would join in. Titus lowered his voice once he had repeated the words a couple of times.

"Your ma is looking fat today." Luke's heart sank. Why did Titus goad him like this?

"Let's say the words once more, Titus. I don't want to get into trouble."

"Your ma is looking fat today."

Luke coloured hotly. "I didn't mean those words. Practice the Latin."

"Your mother's looking fat today. I don't know how to say it in Latin. Shall we ask Master Barton?"

Luke's hand balled itself into a tight fist which met Titus on the nose with more force than Luke realised he had. Blood spouted from Titus' nose immediately, his screech of indignation and pain disturbing the working boys.

Matthias was over them in an instant, grasping each boy by his tabard.

"What on earth is going on?" he demanded, angrily. Luke glared at his tormentor but closed his lips in a thin line, biting the inside of his cheek as he did so.

Titus dabbed ineffectively at his nose, making more mess as the blood flowed down his chin and dripped onto his tunic.

"What is the meaning of this, Luke?"

Luke dropped his head to avoid meeting Matthias' eyes and folded his lips tightly.

"I will ask you once more, Luke."

Luke remained silent. Matthias sighed inwardly. He would not have had this confrontation with Luke if he could have avoided it, but he would not allow such behaviour to go unpunished. He summoned Alice from her curtained room to attend to Titus, now grizzling miserably. Matthias did not meet her eyes as he took up the switch, never yet used in his school. The room was quiet, hushed, breathless with dreadful anticipation.

"I will ask you just one more time, Luke, to explain this assault on Titus."

Luke remained stubbornly silent.

"Do you have anything to say, master Titus?"

"He just hit me...for no reason. We were practising our Latin...he just hit me."

Alice led him away, unable to watch whilst Luke took his punishment at Matthias' hand.

Afterwards, Matthias found himself shaking; he had never had occasion to use the switch on any of his scholars, and he wished it had been anyone other than Luke. He had been as gentle as he could, administering as few strokes as he was able, and Luke had not cried. He had returned to his place in a daze, shock written on his face. Matthias had deliberately not asked him to recite his Latin, feeling Luke had suffered enough for one afternoon. He noticed Ezekiel's boys took Luke with them as they waited for their father to collect them at the end of the session. When Ezekiel had left with the boys, he noticed Luke creep into the barn to see Martin. His demeanour was that of a beaten animal, and Matthias felt terrible.

Alice had mopped Titus' nose and stemmed the flow. She had instructed Davy on how to explain the incident to his father and now came in search of Matthias.

"Was that really necessary, Matthias?"

"Would you have me treat Luke any different to any of the others, Alice? When he first joined the school he was only four years old and things would have been different, but now he is a scholar. He must be treated the same as any other. I cannot have behaviour like that in the classroom."

Alice was silent. She understood the logic of Matthias' actions, but she was hurt for both of them. She wanted to find Luke and cradle him in her arms, comfort his sad heart and make everything alright. She wanted to touch Matthias gently and tell him that he had no choice, that he had given Luke a chance to explain and that she understood his dilemma. In the event, she did neither. She turned back to her teaching room to clean slates and prepare for the next day without a word to either of them.

Edric was satisfied with his temporary apprentice. True, he appeared to know more about wood and carving than he would have expected an apprentice to know, but he was sober, worked quietly and was happy to measure wood for choir seats under which Edric would carve the fantastic misericords...mercy seats for the monks to lean on as they sung their night offices.

He made no effort to make friendly overtures to others working in the great Abbey and seemed very concerned one morning to report to Edric that there appeared to be a chisel missing....one which had been put safely away the previous night. The next day he frowningly reported an auger missing. He was, however, having genuine trouble with toothache. Edric noticed after a few days had passed with no more reports of missing tools that the new apprentice had a very swollen jaw. Never a talkative man, he was even less so, and was clearly in much pain.

"You need to have that pulled." Edric told him. "There's a good barber surgeon just outside Sherborne...lives on the track by St. Cuthbert's church, near Oborne."

His apprentice declined to start with; he did not wish to use his stolen silver for such things, but as the pain grew to unbearable proportions, he was forced to use some of his ill-gotten coin to seek the said barber surgeon.

At first, he thought he might find a cheaper deal on the streets of Sherborne, but the town was much smaller than the one from which he had fled, and no such thing was apparent.

He tramped sullenly out of Sherborne towards the track which led to Oborne, cradling his face in his hood, nearly mad with the pain. He could feel the swelling, feel the throb as he trudged along the mud filled lane.

The barber surgeon's house was a fine one, set apart a little from the track...worth robbing probably, thought the man, eyeing up the roof, the window catches, a little outbuilding half attached to the house. Easy access through that outbuilding was his thought as he lifted the heavy knocker and let it sound through the house.

He was led in to a small room at the front of the house by a serving girl of healthy proportions, and very soon the barber surgeon appeared himself.

It was obvious that the tooth had to be pulled. Ezekiel Jacobson regarded the patient carefully, named a price, accepted his coin and settled him in a hard wooden chair with a bar in front of him instructing him to grip the bar and brace his legs against the wall.

The inside of the man's mouth was rank and swollen, pus festering from the infected tooth. Ezekiel was pleased that he did not have a beard, for saliva was already dribbling down his chin. A rough cloth was placed round the patient to protect his clothes…well cut clothes Ezekiel noticed, not at all in keeping with the general sullen, rude attitude of the man. Perhaps that was all due to his pain.

Cloves came first to attempt to dull the pain, then a swift wrench with the cleansed pliers, a twist, a roar of surprise and the tooth was out, pus underneath bubbling out freely. Ezekiel used a soft pad of wool to press gently on the wound, cleaning the mess from the discharge, pressing gently to stem the flow of blood.

"That shouldn't trouble you again," Ezekiel told him.

The man grunted, sore in his mouth and his head. The less he spoke the less pain he had…and he wanted to get away from this place. He had felt safe in the Abbey, alone with his work, just moving backwards and forwards from his lodging. He felt somehow exposed here, away from the bigger town. A man such as this might have cause to remember him if anything else should go wrong.

As soon as he had earned enough silver, he intended to move East, possibly even beyond the Narrow Sea where he would not be known. The work in the Abbey was ideal for him…just what he liked…just what he was good at.

As he left the house, he turned to print the image of the position of the doors and windows on his mind. A heavy oak door, well latched; small windows, glassed but he had spotted one with a loose catch on the ground floor. This front door had led into a widening hallway, several doors leading further into the house. He had noticed as he left that in the hall there was a pewter platter on a small chest on which had rested two stiletto daggers with jewelled handles, arranged crossed over each other in a pattern - an unsuspecting householder who liked to display his ornaments – except these were hardly ornaments. They had looked like serviceable Italian stiletto daggers and the man was tempted to lift one as he left. No matter – he would remember and lift one in the future when he had need of it.

He nursed his sore jaw as he marched back along the track towards Sherborne, sore, but no longer in that maddening circle of pain. One of those daggers would fit very nicely down the side of his boot, he thought, as he entered the Abbey to continue his work with Edric.

There was a coolness between Alice and Matthias which did not go unnoticed by Martin or Davy.

Martin tried to engage Luke in some simple tasks in the barn with him, but Luke was lack-lustre and low in spirit. Sir Tobias called on them in jovial mood to find them quiet and contemplative.

Alice unfolded the story to her father when Matthias was out in the yard with the scholars.

"Whilst I'm sure Matthias regrets taking that path now, at the time there had to be some action, Alice. Discipline is very important, and Luke has to learn that life is not a primrose path."

"How can we resolve this, Father?"

"Is that the whole story, my dear?"

"No. Luke appears unable to accept Matthias as a father figure. He does all he can to irritate, and Matthias has striven to contain his feelings. He would love Luke, care for him, accept him totally, but Luke does all he can to keep a distance. I accused Matthias of jealousy…I do so wish I had not spoken; Matthias is not a man with any spite in his nature. It was unseemly. Matthias was attempting a fatherly opinion on his behaviour which I admit has begun to affect us all, and I rejected the conversation. It has driven a wedge between us."

Sir Tobias frowned, cupping his chin in his hand and leaning on the table with his other arm. The bench creaked a little as he shifted his weight.

"Let me borrow Luke for a day or two. I will take him into Sherborne to see the builders of the Abbey and Almshouse at work. He can ride his pony beside me...we will take William with us and have a good day out. He can choose some little thing from the market and we will call in to see Thomas Copeland."

Alice agreed somewhat reluctantly. She was not certain why she felt reluctant, but when telling Matthias of the plan she realised what had made her so. Matthias was quick to point out that Luke was being treated differently from the other scholars by missing a day for a jaunt with his Grandfather. He, Matthias, was of the opinion that the difficulties would ease themselves if they were patient. However, Alice had agreed, and Luke was relieved to be away from Barton Holding for a time.

Sir Tobias and William called to collect him, and Davy had his pony saddled ready. Matthias did insist that the party were away from the house before the other scholars arrived and felt very uncomfortable doing so, but he stuck to his principles - Luke could not be seen to be specially treated so the day was to be low key and gone before the other scholars arrived.

Sir Tobias had no official business in Sherborne that day, so he and William allowed Luke to wander through the busy market street, smelling the baking, the leather, the offal, the smoke from fires, all mingled together in a cacophony of smells. Sir Tobias was recognized by many and Luke was proud to be with him. He had not realised how well respected his grandfather was.

He was less pleased, however, when they called on Thomas Copeland. Thomas was advancing in years and had a sterner appearance than Matthias, although in reality he was a gentle soul, totally committed to the teaching of the boys in the school which was run in absentia by the monks at the Abbey, who employed Thomas.

The house, at the bottom of Cheap Street, was considerably larger than Matthias' schoolroom, and far more formal. The boys boarded with a dame in the house next door, owned by the Abbey and refurbished recently to extend the Abbey school. Thomas greeted Sir Tobias and Luke formally, showed Luke the schoolrooms, boys industriously learning passages of Latin tract with a young monk.

"The Abbot has lent us Brother Jerome to help the boys with their disciplines," Thomas explained.

"It has been a great help as we have expanded the school recently." He looked kindly at Luke.

"So, you will be part of us next year, Master Luke. How will you like that?"

Luke tried to stand upright and meet the Master's eyes but he found himself shuffling his feet and unable to give more than a single syllable answer. He was glad when they left, but he could see from Sir Tobias' face that his answer to Thomas Copeland had not delighted his grandfather.

"A few years ago, you would have been expected to live with another family to learn how to become a squire and perform page duties, Luke. Times are changing now, and education in such schools as Master Copelands will serve you better. You have done well with Matthias. You will enjoy Master Copeland's school, too. There will be scholars there with whom you can form long friendships."

Luke remained silent, striving to force his mouth to smile politely.

William joined them outside the school, wanting to show Luke the remnants of the Abbey fire. Sir Tobias paused to speak to a friend, and William and Luke crossed the street and entered the narrow lane towards the Abbey. William pointed to the scaffolding, still in place.

"See, Luke...the wooden pieces are roped together securely so the labourers can reach the places where the fire has damaged the stonework."

Luke looked up at the damaged Abbey in awe. There were workmen on the first level, reached by a wooden ladder fixed to the outside of the scaffolding, with blocks of stone on their shoulders, taken from a large leather bucket hoisted up aloft. The bucket would only hold one block at a time, and Luke could understand how time consuming this work must be. They entered the Abbey, turning right as they entered, leaving the chapel of All Hallows on their left.

Part of the Abbey was silent, untouched by fire, unsullied by the dust and detritus of building. As they neared the choir William stopped, and pointed out the fan vaulted roof, stained red slightly from the flames of the fire. The twelve corbels were carved with great elaboration; it made Luke's neck ache to study them. He left William gazing upwards before dropping to his knees in prayer. Sir Tobias had stopped further to look at the progress on the almshouse, so Luke wandered timidly onwards, finding himself alone with the noise of the masons now distant. A hand descended on his shoulder and made him jump. A man holding a chisel stood behind him, not unfriendly looking, but certainly another workman of some kind.

"What are you doing here, young sir?"

"I'm with my grandsire, looking at the work."

"Come with me and I'll show you another kind of work."

Luke followed the man somewhat uncertainly, and found himself watching an older man carefully gouging wood very delicately, making wood carvings in the shape of real people. Luke watched with excitement as the careful, meticulous work of the wood carver began to take shape. Already he could see eyes, the head dress of a woman - he moved closer to see the strokes of the tool. The master carver was on his knees the better to have a purchase on the work; he seemed oblivious of his admirers, leaving the watching man free to choose a tool from the open pouch of tools on the ground behind Edric. His furtive movements attracted Luke's attention. As he pocketed the tool, his eyes met Luke's, rounded in disbelief. The child had seen the theft. Oh well, he was but a child - who would believe him, if indeed there was anyone to tell?

William found Luke a little later, still watching spellbound and led him reluctantly out into the nave, away from his new-found friend the apprentice, to where Sir Tobias was waiting. Edric completed the nose of the woman and turned to his apprentice.

"That child may do us some good with the Abbot. His Grandfather is the Coroner."

The man felt a chill fear overcome him at the words. This most recent theft could be his undoing.

Chapter 4

.......and Spoil the Child

His grandfather is the Coroner. The words sounded over and over again in his head. He cursed himself for choosing that particular moment to lift the tool; he cursed himself for his friendly overture to the child. How could he possibly know that the child was related to the Coroner of all people - and the child had seen him take and pocket the tool.

What should he do now? The answer was plain - he must move on, and swiftly, before the thefts were made known by the carver and the child spoke up. He would move East, towards Shaftesbury and then onwards to a seaport.

He had no idea where the Coroner lived...probably somewhere in Sherborne, which must mean the child also lived nearby. He must move fast.

In his short time in this small town he had acquired some worthwhile items of clothing, silver coin and some silver plate which could be exchanged in a different town. He did not dare try to exchange it here. The stakes were high for him – he had killed a man – burned his house - raped his woman – used his friend's sister as a cover - he was determined not to be caught. He had put distance between his crime and his person. How foolish it would be to be taken just for the theft of a tool. Tools were value to him; they would provide good cover for him as an itinerant carpenter as he moved on.

He bundled his belongings carefully together and left the town the next morning, before daybreak, unseen by anyone. His simple broken-down shelter was in a part of the town which had been devastated by the plague some years ago, and the buildings left to crumble. He took as many of his stolen items as possible, and left the rest partly concealed by a fallen bulk of timber.

He was glad he had taken careful note of the house of the barber surgeon, for he remembered the knife on the table... recalled the loose window catch and the outhouse. His plan was to watch the house carefully, enter, help himself to just the dagger and then move swiftly on. He needed to be armed for a journey.

Ezekiel Jacobson had calls to make that day; he saddled his mare after delivering the boys to school and left the house with his bag of instruments and ointments. Martha and her maidservant were occupied with harvesting herbs at the back of the house, so the man found it easier than he had anticipated to enter and remove the lethally slim Italian stiletto from the hall. He felt happier now he was armed again. His next aim was to acquire a mode of transport. He certainly did not intend to spend all his time trudging these muddy tracks on foot.

Edric was disappointed to find his apprentice missing from work that morning. He was even more dismayed to discover another tool gone from his collection - tools were his life blood and he could not afford to be without them. The work was too delicate to have to use poor quality tools. When he realised that his new found apprentice was not just late but actually gone, he sought the Abbot's bailiff.

"The Coroner's grandson, you say?" the bailiff muttered, scratching his head.

"He's but a child, Carver, why would he steal a tool?"

"He was there with my temporary apprentice - who else could it have been?"

"What about the apprentice himself?"

Edric thought of the other missing tools and cursed himself for his stupidity.

"And he's not appeared for work today. How dense I have been!"

"Have other tools been lost, Carver?"

"Yes, but the new apprentice reported them to me…I had no cause for suspicion."

The bailiff shook his head disbelievingly. He was one who distrusted everyone.

"You may need to see if your young apprentice is recovered and forget this man. He will be long gone but I will inform the constables, though I fear it is too late to apprehend him."

Luke was back in school the next day. Sir Tobias had not questioned him about his behaviour; rather he had sought to offer him a day away from Barton Holding as a respite from whatever was going on in his mind.

Matthias and Alice were still cool with each other, polite and business like rather than warm and affectionate. Matthias felt this keenly. He believed he had dealt with Luke fairly as he saw it; he could not believe that Alice would want him favoured above the other scholars. Alice for her part was unsure how to resolve matters. She was beginning to understand the difference between the life Matthias led and the life she had led with Allard or in her father's house.

Luke endured the day well, staying close to the Jacobson boys when not in the school room. For once the day was fine, a late Summer sun weakly attempting to dry up the sodden ground of recent heavy rain. Luke sat on the fence in the sun, watching Davy trot off towards the village with his cohort of scholars to meet their escorts. The Jacobson boys had just left and Luke was alone.

He idly considered finding Martin but noticed a man waving to him from the direction of the main track. Luke hesitantly slid down from the fence and ambled towards the waving figure. As he drew closer, he recognized the apprentice he had spoken to in the Abbey the previous day. The man was smiling, although in what a more astute person would have described as a wolfish manner.

"Can you help me, lad? Is that your pony?"

The man had experienced little trouble in tracing the whereabouts of Luke and planned exactly what he intended.

Luke looked to where he was pointing. "Yes. That's my pony. Why do you want to know?"

"I'm considering buying a steed for my lad. Can you show him to me?"

Luke thought he seemed friendly enough, forgetting that he had witnessed a theft. Luke looked round for Davy - not yet back from the village - or Martin -busy in the barn -or Matthias - working in the schoolroom. The afternoon was wearing on, the man was friendly he thought proudly - I can do this myself.

He felt quite grown up as he unhitched the beast, already saddled by Davy ready to escort Luke out before supper, and showed the man how well he could walk, trot and canter.

"I'll get up behind you and see for myself," and with no further conversation Luke found himself pushed further forward in his saddle with the strong hands of the apprentice round his waist, holding him firmly. What happened next was for Luke, little short of a nightmare.

The ride was uncomfortable, fast, wild and desperate. They left the track and plunged downhill into untended woodland, branches and twigs cruelly catching their faces, tearing at their clothes and making the pony skittish. Luke's breath came in gasps as he held on to the reins, the apprentice's bony hands clasped round his own the better to control the frightened pony. They rode in this manner for half an hour, Luke sobbing now, pleading for the man to turn back, aghast and terrified at the manner in which he had been fooled by a simple request, and his own folly in not seeking help.

When they stopped it was only because the pony, lathered and wild eyed with hysterical fear, the whites of her eyes rolling, came to a shuddering halt. Luke slipped from the saddle and sank to the ground.

"Take me home, please. Don't ever ride like that again."

The apprentice had turned into a menacing, gaunt figure as he towered over Luke, who found himself suddenly retching with fear on the muddy floor of the woodland.

"No, brat. You won't be going home. I need you for a while, and I need this beast. We have a journey to make. Get on your feet. We'll rest this poor animal - she can walk for a bit until we find a place to stop for the night."

Luke managed to sound defiant, briefly.

"Matthias will come after you. They'll find me. My grandfather will hang you. He is the Coroner."

His words sounded hollow and childish, but the apprentice gave an ugly, coarse laugh and slapped Luke across the face viciously.

"That is exactly why you will not be going home, brat. We have a journey to make, and if you do as I say, you may live... if not, there are plenty of places where a body will never be found."

Alice and Matthias, silent as the grave together, left the schoolroom and moved into the cheerful room Alice had taken such pleasure in creating. They expected Luke to be there, waiting for supper, but there was no sign of him.

"He must be with Martin," Alice murmured.

I'll go and find him," Matthias volunteered, leaving the room.

Dear Lord, he thought, as he crossed the yard towards the barn, how has it come to this so quickly, we are being so polite to each other and I can't seem to put anything right.

Luke was not with Martin, and Martin had not seen Luke since the scholars had left. The last time he was seen was when he waited with the Jacobsons by the fence. Martin hobbled from the barn, concerned that Luke may have run away a second time.

As the two men stood together outside the barn, perplexed, Davy returned from the village.

"Master, have you allowed Luke to ride out on his own?" Davy asked, uncertainly. "I left the pony saddled and ready for riding with Luke before supper. The pony is gone."

"God's blood!" Matthias exclaimed, angrily. "What do I have to do to atone for beating a pupil who attacks another in class...what have I done to deserve the strain this has put on my new family?"

He turned on his heel and strode back to the house, calling for Alice as he did so. His eyes filled with furious tears as he confronted Alice in his frustration, bewilderment and pain.

"Your son has repeated his antics once more. I cannot have this disruption. Alice. What have I done that causes Luke to behave so?"

"You know what you have done, Matthias. You beat him in front of his fellow scholars."

Her voice was cold; she was not afraid to stand up to his words.

"You want him to be treated as a special case, Alice? He attacked another scholar and apparently with no justification. He was allowed the chance to defend his action. There was no defence."

Matthias' eyes were dark with fury.

"I note you describe him as 'my' son. Is there no feeling in you that he should now be part of you?" Her breath came unevenly as she stood her ground before this new, angry version of her husband.

"My willingness to treat him as part of my family was always there, Alice. He is destroying it; I don't understand why. God knows I have made every attempt to embrace him as a son. Now I have to saddle up the mare and go to fetch him from Purse Caundle, because that is undoubtedly where he has gone."

Matthias turned on his heel and would have left, but the sour words between them were not yet over.

"And what will you say to my Father? That Luke is a disruption you wish to be rid of? You can't wait for him to be with Master Copeland."

"The trouble is deep rooted, my lady. Luke has led a pampered life with a spoiled mother."

Words escaped from him in his blind temper.

"Deep rooted in you, also. If Luke was your natural son would you have beat him so?"

"For attacking a fellow scholar, yes, undoubtedly. Discipline is breaking down all around us. Those who are not able to comply will be our undoing."

"Pampered, you call me? How dare you!" Alice gasped at the feeling that there was some fault in herself; never had that been suggested to her before - not even when Allard had deserted her.

"Oh, I dare. The truth hurts no-one if you're willing to accept it."

"The truth with you, Matthias, is that you have a cold core. Natural warmth is denied you."

An icy hand crept round his heart at her words, returning him to the bad old days he thought he had left behind.

"And you are too cosseted to accept the harsh reality of life. Do you want Luke to grow up feeling that he can always rely on you to cushion his failings? Has he inherited his natural father's failings?"

"Allard was a brave leader of men. I would be pleased if Luke followed him in that way."

"Well he certainly has no chance of that if he cannot accept simple discipline."

Matthias turned sharply and left Alice trembling with unspent rage.

How dare he include Allard in this unlooked for argument? Why did Luke behave in this way? Was Matthias right to chastise him as he had done? Pampered? What did he mean? It was the first time Matthias had lost his temper so utterly and both their words had barbs which caused pain.

She was shaking uncontrollably now he had left the room; she wanted to smash something to relieve her anger. Crossing to the fire grate they had so proudly installed, she gripped the flower petals displayed there and crushed them fiercely in her fists, tearing at the blooms with an intensity she hadn't known she had.

She heard Matthias shout for his horse with a roughness in his voice that she had not heard before and watched him ride out of the gate in the direction of Purse Caundle. Later, on her knees in the nearby church, she prayed for her marriage, her son and her husband as the tears fell on her clasped hands.

Matthias did not return until after dark. He, Sir Tobias and William had been out all evening searching for the child. Matthias had felt too ashamed to speak of the fierce argument he and Alice had endured, but Sir Tobias was a perceptive man; he guessed harsh words had passed between them and did not pry. With unrest in the countryside, poor weather, returning and marauding soldiers, William had agreed to stay out all night, retracing their steps, dismounting and searching ditches, disused barns, calling all the time and hoping for a distant response.

Daylight brought no result. Alice was beside herself with grief, despair and remorse. Davy gathered a small group of villagers who would down tools and search again, going in different directions. Matthias had been so sure that Luke had ridden to Purse Caundle that he had not given any thought to other areas.

Martin was detailed to school duties once more, allowing Matthias to join the search. He had spent a sleepless night, lying beside Alice who kept her body rigid and isolated. Matthias did not dare touch her for fear of re-igniting the row between them, still hovering over their heads.

The scholars were subdued; they understood that bad things could happen out in the countryside, unprotected citizens were robbed, beaten, stripped of their clothes and possessions, and it was not unusual for traveling bands of ragged dispossessed men and women to steal livestock, even healthy children if they thought they might have a use for them, or they could sell them on as slaves. Although no such gangs had been reported hereabouts, there was always a first time.

Titus was particularly subdued. He lingered beside Martin at the close of day, waiting for Martin to pick up his crutches.

"Sir, have they found Luke?" he faltered. Martin was surprised by his demeanour. Titus was usually one of the more strident scholars and it occurred to Martin that Titus might have some light to shed on Luke's disappearance.

"Not yet, Titus. You sometimes work with Luke - do you have any idea of what might be in his mind?"

Titus lowered his head and muttered something indistinct.

"You said what, Titus? I didn't hear you properly."

Titus repeated his admission. "There was a reason why Luke hit me. It wasn't fair that Luke was beaten, he just wouldn't say."

"What was that reason, Titus?"

There fell an awkward silence. Titus reddened. Martin waited, shifting his weight onto his better leg.

"I can't stand waiting for too long, Titus. My leg will give out."

Titus gave a watered-down explanation of the conversations he had had with Luke. Martin's perception was crisper than Titus' mumbled confession, and he was able to fill in the gaps with accuracy.

"Very unkind, Titus. Master Barton would be ashamed of you. Luke is younger than you and you have spoiled his chances of feeling part of a new family. It is not seemly to comment on Mistress Barton in that way. It is a lowly way to perceive her. What would your father say if he knew of this conversation?"

Titus was silent. He knew his father would be shamed by his son's dishonesty in not speaking up at the time of the beating, let alone the comments regarding Mistress Barton's condition.

"You must speak with Master Barton and confess all this to him, Titus, but I think it should wait until Luke has been found. They have much to concern them until they can find Luke."

Martin wondered privately how he could convey this information to Matthias, especially as it did not have any light to shine on where he might have fled to. Titus left to return home, families all solicitously offering help and advice in the search for the child.

The searches had revealed nothing. Luke seemed to have completely disappeared.

Chapter 5

Fruitless Searching

Sherborne was preparing for the big Summer Gooseberry fair. Travellers and traders came from miles around to this annual event which was one of the highlights of the town. It was a six-day event and attracted hundreds of traders from miles around. There would be exotic fruits, alluring perfumed goods, magic toys made from wood with moving parts painted garishly - freshly baked buns, apples dipped in honeyed syrup, and plenty of ale to drink, spiced cider from local folk, and best of all, mummers with strange and wonderful plays mounted on carts which would move as they unfolded their stories. It was the last of the fairs except for the Michaelmas fair, and was held at the Green which was at the very top of Cheap Street.

It was now a week since Luke had vanished. No trace of his pony had been found, and Matthias, William, Ezekiel and a cohort of villagers had scoured the surrounding countryside with increasing desperation with little or no success. They had descended the slope where they had found torn bushes, broken twigs and hoofprints, but after a while these had petered out altogether due to increased rains, and the terrain was so steep that it would appear impossible for a beast as unused to rough ground as Luke's little mount to have managed this. Reluctantly they decided the tracks were those of poachers.

Alice was distraught with imaginings of Luke frozen to death, thirst and hunger taking their toll or of finding his body, throat cut, in a ditch which somehow everyone had neglected to search.

Matthias was leaden eyed from lack of sleep, exhausted with worry, ridden with guilt. Somehow, he kept the school running with Martin following his instructions.

Alice would have gone home to Purse Caundle, but her father told her sternly that Barton Holding was her home now, and she should stay there. Alice was unused to hearing her father so stern; Luke and Alice had been Sir Tobias and Lady Bridget's pride and joy for years, but Sir Tobias recognized the fault in himself for spoiling both Alice and Luke, indulging them in the sweetest way, neglecting to remind her that she was enjoying a most comfortable life. All had been done in love, but when tested as she was now, Alice had no resilience.

William and Davy rode together into Sherborne on the first day of the fair. They stabled their horses at Ezekiel's home as the press of people meant they would have found stabling in the town difficult, and walked in to Sherborne, Ezekiel joining them. His boys begged to accompany them, but Martha and Ezekiel exchanged glances and refused them. Ezekiel knew that William and Davy had planned to use their visit to question traders who may have seen something of the child, for it had become obvious that he was not nearby.

The three men split up once they had agreed a meeting place for later, thinking they might cover more ground if they were working singly.

Davy worked his way round to the great cart bedecked with streamers, ribbons and greenery and watched wide-eyed as the simple story of Noah's great flood unfolded. The dove, a white bundle of feathers mounted on a stick, emerged from the cut-out window in the side of the cart, flapped unceremoniously and returned. The third time as expected it carried a green twig in its hooked beak and a cheer went up from the watching crowd. Noah, dressed in a long brown robe and looking thoroughly disinterested in the whole proceedings, announced the end of the rains, and another cheer went up.

The actors emerged on the deck of the ark to take their bow, and Noah jumped down and made for the nearest ale house.

The crowd dispersed and Davy moved on, feeling slightly guilty that he had paused to enjoy the spectacle. However, he did notice that amongst the actors were several children, and although none of them looked distressed, as he imagined Luke would be by now if he had been taken against his will, he examined the faces as they clambered down from the waggon but could see nothing amiss with any of them.

He moved further into the crowd, pausing at various stalls, listening hard for any sounds of dissension. Luke would be far away from here by now he felt sure, and he was not certain how he should approach people who were clearly here to trade and enjoy the rare sunshine in this the wettest of Summers.

William had no such misgivings about speaking to strangers. An older man, more used to tackling difficult matters head on, he kept one hand on his purse as he strode through the crowd. He was here on business; no-one was going to cut his purse from him. He stopped by a booth selling sugared plums, the sweetness of the spices and warm honey assailing his nostrils delightfully. He purchased one, dribbling its sweetness down the twig on which it was speared. All in his mouth at once was the only way to prevent him from smearing the honeyed juices all over his hands, so he was unable to converse with the vendor until he had finished the treat. He licked his fingers before he spoke.

"That was good...where do you hail from?"

"Evesham, we work the fairs once the plums are ripe for picking...this is the furthest South we come."

"I'm looking for a lad. Disappeared from home a week or so ago. Seen nothing amiss as you travel?"

The plum seller shook his head.

"'fraid not. All seems quiet this season. We don't all travel together, but no, I've no news for you."

William moved on. A puppet master was setting up his show with a gaggle of youth watching, jeering now and again as the puppeteer struggled to erect his stage. He was a small man with a shortened arm on his right side, making the booth hard to steady on his own. As it toppled dizzily to one side, the youths booed once more. William stepped forward to hold the side of the fabric to enable the man to insert the rods holding the staging together. The youths lost interest and moved on.

William repeated his question. The answer was the same. He sighed and moved on again.

Ezekiel was on the far side of The Green by now and having pushed and shoved his way through the crowd of people, he was on the edge of the fair where it was less busy. There were several young men showing off their skills at a simple trestle set up by the guild master. One of these was the apprentice who had been injured, and who was now ready to return to his place in the Abbey. He was showing his newly learned skill of smoothing wood, marking out a simple pattern and gouging carefully to lift the wood to allow the pattern to sit proud.

Ezekiel watched him for a minute or two before he noticed the scar on his forehead running through his hair. It was still very visible, although healing well.

"You didn't gouge your own head then?" he asked with a smile.

"I was set upon in the Abbey," he replied, "by a stranger who fled and evaded the hue and cry."

The resentment was clear in the young voice.

"How unfriendly," Ezekiel commented, and was about to move on when another apprentice chipped in with another part of the story.

"There was another man who took Peterkin's place while he was recovering. He didn't last long either. He was stealing Master Edric's tools."

"It appears we are all at the mercy of thieves...." agreed Ezekiel, quietly, "I had a thief in my house recently....one of my beautiful decorative daggers which were a reminder of my time in Italy.....just gone without any trace. A very clever thief."

"There's been a lot of thieving in Sherborne just lately," the young apprentice volunteered. "Silver, garments, jewellery... No-one has been safe."

The guildmaster noticed the conversation and moved over to listen. The apprentices were demonstrating their skills, not selling. He had six or seven of them in various stages of their apprenticeship, and he was anxious that they did not sell, lest they have to pay the fair's fee which would go to the Bishop, as did all stallage fees for the Gooseberry Fair.

"The apprentices have interested you, sir?"

"Some good work, but we were simply condoning the thefts that have been happening in the town and looking at the pretty pattern on this young man's head."

The guild master scowled at the mention of thefts.

"Master Edric apparently had several tools taken by a fellow working for him who then left in a great hurry. He thought at first it was the young boy who had been watching him, but that turned out to be the grandson of the Coroner. It was so unlikely to have been him. He can't be more than six or seven Summers old -"

Ezekiel stopped him in mid-sentence.

"The child is missing. When did you see him with this man?"

But the guildmaster could tell him no more, and suggested he seek out the Master Carver, Edric.

Ezekiel hurried down Cheap Street towards the Abbey, but the carver was not there. Gooseberry Fair was a great holiday for most local people, and although they did not expect to have all the six days free of work, they certainly spent the first day at the fair. Great fairs were a chance to stock up on goods not often seen in the local trading places and to exchange news and commodities with each other. The town was packed with people; ale houses and hostelries would do good business - beds would be full and heads sore by the second day. Ezekiel could find no-one who knew where Edric lived, but he was directed to a small ale house where he was reliably informed that he would find the carver.

Edric was crouched on an upturned barrel, hands clasped round a blackjack of ale. He was not an easy man to pin down, but he gave an account of the original attack on Peterkin as well as an indignant telling of the theft of tools and the disappearance of his new helper. Edric recalled that he had mentioned that the child watching him work was the grandson of the Coroner. After that, the attention of the man had wandered, he'd appeared agitated and he had not returned to work the next day.

"Mayhap he knew he'd be identified as the thief," Edric opined, thoughtfully, taking a final swig of his ale. Ezekiel put a silver piece on the table nearby. "You've given me good information," he told him, "put that towards the cost of your lost tools."

"Thank you, Sir – the young lad was interested in the work I was doing – tell me if you find him. I lost a day's work from the wretch – he had to find the barber surgeon for a tooth extraction, - so he wasn't such a good investment. Glad Peterkin is mended now.

Ezekiel gasped.

"I've seen the man then! I am the barber surgeon – he came to my house. I extracted his tooth – a surly man with a slight twist in one eye? "

"The same,"agreed Edric.

"And he stole from you? I had a decorative stiletto dagger stolen from me very recently…he would have seen it in my house…."

Excited, Ezekiel met Davy and William and made for home with all haste.

Alice and Matthias had led the household to Mass the next day. As she knelt to pray for the safety of her son, Alice begged forgiveness for her weakness, prayed for a return of her love for Matthias, strove to contain her tears as she fought to stifle sobs while Matthias knelt beside her in silence, unable to reach out his hand to give her support. He was himself in the grip of a fear that he would not be able to look on Alice with the same feelings of love that he had felt before. She had wanted Matthias to indulge Luke and ignore his behaviour in class, when had it been another scholar, she would have encouraged the punishment. He felt she was now holding him responsible for the disappearance of the child, blaming him for Luke's strange behaviour.

Martin, standing balanced on his crutches behind them, wondered anew how he could begin to explain to Matthias what he had learned from Titus. He had not done so because he did not think it bore any relevance to Luke's disappearance, but he was beginning to think maybe it should be told, however much hurt was caused, and there is certainly much hurt there, he thought, observing Matthias' carefully turned head away from Alice, his green eyes blindly staring at the glassed windows of the church whilst Alice, shoulders braced against the sobs she sought to subdue, bent over the book of hours clutched in her hand, looking fragile and wretched.

The host was elevated; Martin bowed his head, unable to see a way through the morass of misery that had engulfed the little family of whom he had become so fond, and to whom he owed so much.

After Mass it was a sober party meeting in the empty schoolroom.

Ezekiel joined them; Alice insisted on being present, eager to hear first-hand what the men might have discovered. She had scrubbed away her tears and tried to appear stronger, ashamed of her despair.

Ezekiel began, "This was a man intent on theft, and the sudden realisation that the watching child may have seen the action...and worse still, was the grandson of yourself, Sir Tobias. He will hang for theft He also caused serious injury to the apprentice of the Master Carver in the Abbey."

"It appears to me that he will thieve again as he travels - he may be on foot or he may be mounted. Luke's pony is gone … is that a coincidence? Possibly Luke himself rode off on his pony but we cannot be sure," the Coroner mused.

The worry for Luke's safety was eating into him, but he was now further troubled by the lack of visible warmth between Alice and Matthias.

"Could Luke have tried to go to Salisbury to find his other grandfather?" Alice ventured, hesitantly. Matthias was startled. "Why would you think so, Alice?" His tone was chilly; there was no eye contact between them, and Alice did not lift her eyes to the assembled company.

"I don't know," she faltered, unwilling to divulge that Luke had asked her to describe his father to him recently.

Sir Tobias was more forthright.

"Has Luke asked about him, Alice?"

Alice was reluctant to reply.

"Alice! I'm asking you a question," Sir Tobias rasped.

Alice was startled at her father's tone. He had never spoken to her like that before, - and in front of other people. Was she such a spoilt woman, she wondered, feeling sick as she breathed deeply and faced her father's troubled eyes?

"Yes," she answered, hardly able to make her voice heard. What was happening to her? She had been so strong a few months ago, - now she was falling to pieces for no reason except a growing realisation that her life had undergone a change which she had not anticipated and could not control.

"What did you tell him, Alice?"

"I explained that he was a soldier, a captain, and that he was brave."

"Is that all?" Matthias' voice sounded very distant.

"Why would it be any different?" Alice responded with a return of some spirit.

Matthias bent his head to hide the pain in his eyes. He felt he had no place in the world of Alice and Luke - that all he had striven for had turned to dust. Alice came from a different world; he had fooled himself that she would match his spirit of endeavour. She had fallen at the first hurdle. He was impotent in the help he could offer.

"I told him that his father was a captain in the King's army in France who had met his death there.

He asked me if his father had loved him. That wasn't so easy to answer because I don't really know.

Allard walked away from us willingly, but I was able to say that he was pleased when Luke was born."

Alice looked more directly at Matthias as she added this detail, gathering what little strength she had.

Matthias nodded curtly, acknowledging her explanation.

Alice shrank into herself again, suddenly unable to comprehend what was happening to them. How could it be that after such initial happiness, this had turned so sour? A few days ago she had willingly stood with Elizabeth learning how to brew and bake - things she had never had to do in her father's house, nor in the home of her first husband. She had, she conceded to herself in that moment, lived a cosseted life and her married state had opened a different lifestyle. She loved teaching her young scholars, was grateful to her father for his liberated thinking which allowed her to learn things many women would never have access to, had played at being the mistress of Barton Holding, adored her young son - was love for a son deeper than love for a husband? She tried to remind herself that if it were not for Matthias, she would have been wed to an older man. She remembered how she had begged Matthias to help her, not really knowing herself what she expected him to do and being grateful when he had offered her a partnership in the school. Perhaps she should have just kept it as it was - a partnership.

Sir Tobias, Ezekiel and Martin soon left Alice and Matthias alone in their solar, silence deepening between them.

"I am a disappointment to you, Matthias. We should have remained partners."

"My life is more different than you had expected, Alice. I don't have cooks, serving girls, a steward. Davy and Elizabeth are the closest I have to a cook and a steward, and I have no desire to change that."

Alice struggled to speak calmly, fought to control her rising panic. She looked round the room she had created with so much pleasure and excitement just a few months ago and saw herself as a pampered child instead of a mature woman. Had she been playing at being married to a man whose life was so different from her own? Her father had made it plain to her that she belonged here now. In her heart, Alice knew that this was really where she wanted to be, but she needed to leave her old self behind and grow into her new role. She remembered how good it had felt to lie beside Matthias when he had been suffering from marsh fever, how complete it had made them both. Where had that all gone?

"I am trying to belong to your life. I realise that being married to you is the hardest thing I've ever done. Without understanding it, I have lived a spoiled life. Now I must face my demons and accept my chosen path. But Luke is my beloved son, who was my saving grace when Allard went to war. Mother and father adore him - they are suffering too. How can this be happening? Where is he?"

A cry of despair broke from her as she spoke. Matthias touched her face gently, stroking a curl escaped from her wimple.

"I don't have a place in your world," Matthias said, sadly. "I've tried, Alice. I had no idea it would be so hard."

"Please keep trying, Matthias," she whispered, the lump in her throat rising to choke her words.

"I do want you in my world, and I want to be part of your life. The love I have for Luke is different from the love I have for you."

Matthias turned away from her to hide the rush of relief which flooded his face.

"Some things are too hard to bear. You just have to learn to accept and keep going. We have to face up to some unbearable possibilities, Alice."

Alice bowed her head to hide her tears. She had cried enough, and Matthias would not want a wife who cried at every turn.

"You have been through so much grief that it now sits easily on you. You have faced the worst and emerged whole. I have endured some bad things, but they have always been cushioned by my birth and family - truths have been softened for me, hidden from me. You have had to face such things alone, and it has made you a stronger person. I don't have your strength. I will fail as your wife. I should have remained your partner. I was strong then"

Matthias reached out to touch her hands,

"And you will be strong again, Alice."

Once she would have responded by hugging him tightly in love and gratitude, but now she felt herself to be so far beneath him in spirit that all she could offer was a slight tightening of her fingers on his hand before rising to seek solace outside whilst the sun was still bright.

Matthias was keenly aware of a sense of failure...he was unused to not being able to lift her mood.

Martin watched as Alice wandered aimlessly over to the fence on which Luke had sat waiting with Ezekiel's boys. He set his mind to what he had to do and went into the schoolroom to find Matthias.

Elizabeth was cooking - there was a strange sense of normality in this nightmare they were living in. The fragrance of the stew gave them all a slice of Elizabeth's mantra that life must continue, and what better way to help them than to keep them fed with good pottage.

"I must talk with you, Matthias."

"Can it not wait, Martin? I don't think I can bear any more today."

"No. I must talk with you. I should have spoken days ago, before Luke disappeared."

Matthias looked alarmed and perched uncomfortably on one of the benches, tucking his long legs underneath him.

"This is going to sound intrusive and rude," began Martin, more aware of his station in life than he had ever done. "Titus has been filling Luke's head with stories of the consequences of marital couplings…..of Luke being pushed out of the nest by a new baby….of what might happen to him…….of how just a kiss can cause a quickening…..of disgusting things done between a man and a woman - " he tailed off, afraid he had gone too far but very needful of capturing Matthias' full attention.

"The day you thrashed Luke, Titus told Luke that his mother was looking fat so she must be with child. He wanted to ask you how Luke could say it in Latin."

Silence fell in the schoolroom.

Matthias recalled Luke's stubborn silence, not once but three times. The child had refused to betray his tormentor. And been thrashed for it. By him, Matthias. In front of Titus, who had not owned up.

"How long has this been going on?" Matthias was aghast. He had caned Luke unfairly - there was an explanation for Luke's mistrust of him as a husband and as a father - even as a man.

"Since your marriage, I would guess. Matthias, I am sorry to have to tell you this - it is not my place to pry or judge; when Titus told me I didn't know how to tell you, but it might at least throw some light on why Luke has been so unhappy."

Matthias put his head down on the trestle and wept tears of hopeless frustration, guilt, anger and fear. Where had this unhappy child gone? What had happened to him?

Martin lowered himself down beside Matthias and sat quietly, waiting for the storm to subside.

The news of Luke's disappearance spread through Milborne Port, Oborne and Sherborne, for the Coroner and the schoolmaster were well known and popular in some circles.

Martin postponed his own work to help in the school, and Alice's sad face helped the boys to remember that Luke was one of them and had disappeared. Before Matthias went out once again with William to search further afield he sent for Titus, and what passed between them remained private; Titus was very subdued and thankful that he had not lost his place in the school, for if that had happened, his father would have been very disappointed in him, and Titus did not wish for that.

It was the final day of the Gooseberry Fair when Sir Tobias rode once more into Sherborne, Coroner's work requiring his attention once more.

He held court as usual in the George, close by the edge of the fair. The noise and bustle of the fair made his head ache, hearing the comments of the tithing men was difficult and the felons brought before him were petty cases of a domestic nature. His scribe laboured under misunderstandings due to the hubbub of the nearby cart bearing the players which Davy had watched a few days ago.

Sir Tobias threw his staff down on the oak table in despair.

"Court adjourned. I must take some air."

He stumbled outside into the damp air. The rains had returned overnight and the atmosphere of the fair had been dampened literally as well as physically.

Dressed in warm dark green hose and murray waistcoat, brown boots to his thigh and his dark red robes belted at the waist, he was clearly a personage to be reckoned with; his chain of office round his neck rested lightly against his white linen undershirt proclaiming his importance as a man of justice, and before he had taken more than a few steps, the actor playing Noah jumped heavily off the cart upon which he had been resting between sessions and accosted him, arms akimbo, great legs splayed out, an appeal in his troubled eyes.

"Sir, I am seeking a man who has cruelly wronged my sister. He fled after killing my brother, his wife and their serving girl. My sister stands accused of helping him, shielding him in his escape and is due at the assizes shortly. He fled from the hue and cry most efficiently....it was clearly planned, but I do not believe my sister to be guilty of helping him. He was once my friend, working with me as one of the players on the cart. I hope to find him as the fairs work South. He cannot run for ever. Do you know of any strangers who have come into this town seeking work?"

Sir Tobias took a step back, looking piercingly at the stout fellow.

"If we knew of such a man, we would apprehend him. Your name, fellow? Apart from Noah,"

"My name is Merrik of Bradford-by-Avon. He fled from our place...evaded the hue and cry...stole good silver from our holy church...he has been gone three weeks now and must surely have come South. I am searching for him whenever I have time from this cart, but so far there is no sighting of him."

"There has been a stranger in town, but he was skilled in work and took casual work in the Abbey..."

Merrik's shoulders slumped despairingly. "He would be lying low and very careful to disseminate, Sir Coroner. He is a wood carver...a journeyman in the trade, and a jealous and cunning man. Also a skilled actor."

Sir Tobias grasped Merrik by the arm.

"Come with me...I know of a man who may be able to help us both."

Abandoning his court without so much as a word to his scribe, Sir Tobias led the way down the length of Cheap Street and into the Abbey grounds. He was excited, out of breath with anticipation and anxious to reach Edric for more talk of his temporary apprentice.

Merrik was awed by the Abbey. He had not been inside such a great church before. The cool pillars, stone corbels looking down on him, length of the nave, beginnings of stupendous fan vaulting high above his head dizzied him for a moment, and he stood and gaped, afraid to move in the vast space. Dressed as he was for his part as Noah, he resembled one of the monks, but when he stood in front of the kneeling Edric, on the ground, squinting in the poor light the better to see his work, it was obvious that he had no tonsure, no knotted rope around his waist symbolising poverty, chastity and obedience.

Edric glared at them until he recognized the Coroner. Peterkin was nearby, holding tools, brushing dust away from completed carvings. He stood up, stretching his cramped limbs, easing his back.

"My lord Coroner," he murmured.

"I am sorry to have to ask you to remember again, Master Carver - the man who worked with you. What can you tell us of him?"

"His appearance, sir," Merrik urged him.

Edric scratched his head, shaking fragments of wood shavings onto his rough tunic.

"He was clean shaven..." he began. Merrik interrupted with a quick air of disappointment.

"No – he had a dark beard, the man I am seeking. Waste of time, Coroner."

"Not so fast, Merrik. How easy is it to shave, to cut hair, to change your gait...your clothes? You told me he was an actor. You should know...you are an actor yourself."

The Coroner's intervention made Peterkin bold enough to speak out.

"Sir, when the man asked for work before he struck me, he had a beard and long straggly hair. I do remember that,"

"Well said, young man," applauded Sir Tobias.

"This apprentice was clean shaven," repeated Edric, stubbornly, not understanding.

"What else?" Sir Tobias asked him, patiently.

"A wall eye," muttered Edric, scowling to remember.

"A wall eye?" queried Merrik.

"Eyes not coming together right," explained Edric, impatiently. He needed to press on with his work; he was running behind schedule now.

"That's him!" exclaimed Merrik, shouting in his delight, making an echo round the Abbey.

"Where did he lodge?" asked Sir Tobias, but Edric had no idea.

Together they pressed Edric and Peterkin to remember as much as they could about the man. Peterkin was little use to them – he had been struck in anger and hurt too badly.

As they spoke Sir Tobias became more and more certain that the man had sought out Luke to prevent capture. Merrik's account of the vicious murder of his brother and sister in law was a tale of jealousy, greed and lust, and the doubt thrown on his sister's involvement was an urgent matter. The man needed to be captured and brought to justice.

Sir Tobias had no doubt that the path of this deranged man would include more killing, and he hoped that would not include his beloved grandson. Few things frightened Sir Tobias in his life, but he now felt deep dread for Luke's safety, especially as they had no idea where to look for him.

"How well do you know this man?" Sir Tobias asked him, urgency in his tone.

Merrik explained that until recently, Walter had been part of the players on the cart, a friend of his sister, following his work with wood and carving in between plays, and had caused much dissension and unrest amongst the company of players. He was known to be a man of dangerous mood and few would willingly cross him.

"What makes a man turn into such a devil?" Edric wondered, listening with horror at the thought that he had used such a man.

"Some few years ago, Walter had a son and a wife...they were abducted and killed by a soldier returning from the French wars which had turned the man's brain. He saw their slaughtered bodies lying in pools of blood outside their own house, the woman raped, the child's throat cut. Walter never forgave himself for not being at home that day."

"The Coroner's grandson witnessed the theft of tools from me," Edric explained. "The child is now missing."

"Walter would have searched for him…he is nothing if not cunning. He will be anxious to evade capture. He may use the boy as cover of some kind. I don't believe it is in his nature to kill a child, not with his past history of seeing his own boy killed. He might wish to use the boy as a comfort to him."

"Where might he have fled to?" Sir Tobias wanted to know.

Merrik scratched at his rough costume, sweating under the hessian robe.

"He will make for a port and take ship, I warrant. The boy will be with him. I may be wrong, but my guess is that is what his plan will be."

Walter Woodman, I'm coming after you," declared Sir Tobias, although as yet he had no idea how to find him.

Chapter 6

Penny for a Pony

Ezekiel Jacobson had travelled to Shaftesbury that same day to visit his sister Jenna, now a lay worker in the great Abbey in that hill-top town. Jenna had been the victim of a cruel murder from which she had emerged damaged...slower than she had been, saddened by the loss of her husband, forgetful sometimes, but able to perform menial tasks in the laundry of the Abbey, who had given her succour and nursed her carefully back to a degree of health. She was able to live in her own house once more, but Ezekiel noticed the garden lying neglected, the gate unlatched. Isaac had been very proud of the garden and took care to make sure the gate was latched to prevent pigs, dogs and other livestock from spoiling his plot. He determined to bring his boys over one day soon to help Jenna restore the beauty of the garden. He should come more often – or possibly Jenna might like to move nearer to he and his wife?

After a repast of fresh bread and honey, Jenna and Isaac walked up the hill towards the town, admiring the emerging view of the surrounding countryside as they neared the summit.

Knowing Jenna took a little time now to understand stories, Ezekiel was patient as he told Jenna about the disappearance of Luke. When they reached the top of the hill he sought out John Croxhale, taverner of the Swan, to tell him of the missing child. News spread by word of mouth could bring results, and there were still many pilgrim visitors to Shaftesbury who could spread the word and who might bring news. Sitting in the watery sun outside the hostelry, Ezekiel described Luke and watched carefully as passers-by drifted from the Abbey and continued down towards the markets.

There were many people in the town making good use of the respite in the miserable Summer weather. Ezekiel followed them into the handsome marketplace behind St. Peter's church, taking care to protect Jenna as they walked on the slippery cobbles made treacherous by so much rain. The buzz of the market sounded hollow in Ezekiel's ears as he mused on the child, apparently gone without trace. It seemed very sinister to him, aware as he was of the difficulty of picking up any threads to follow.

They paused at several booths to look at goods and Ezekiel purchased some trinkets for Jenna and Martha. As they turned back to the Abbey, where Jenna was now working, Ezekiel stopped to look at several mounts tethered on the verge, a tinker harnessing them together ready to move on. The last one was lame, seemed broken winded and he guessed may well not make much of a journey before being abandoned. He looked more closely, running his hand across the beast's flanks. The tinker eyed him suspiciously.

"What's your interest, Sir?" he asked nervously, backing away.

"Where did this one come from?" Ezekiel asked him.

"That's no concern of yours, but he wasn't stolen, if that's what you're thinking."

The mount was no longer the fat little pony he once had been, but the marking down the nose and on the fetlocks was identical.

Ezekiel decided. He didn't want confrontation.

"He'll be nothing but trouble to you...he's lame and winded. I'll buy him for my boys and nurse him through it."

The tinker didn't hesitate, but named a higher price than Ezekiel was prepared to pay.

He fingered two silver pieces.

The tinker glanced at them with greed.

"Make it three."

"Who did this mount come from?" Ezekiel queried, allowing suspicion to creep into his voice.

The tinker faltered.

"I'll take the two."

Ezekiel grasped him by one arm.

"Who?"

The tinker winced at the pincer like grip of Ezekiel's fingers and squirmed round to feel for his knife.

Jenna watched in disbelief as her gentle brother became menacing.

"Don't even think about a knife," her brother declared, "describe the man and take the money."

The tinker's eyes shifted uneasily.

"A rough looking man with a young boy. He said they were joining a line of pack ponies to go to the coast. There didn't seem to be anything wrong with that."

"What was the boy looking like?"

"Tired, they had been travelling for a while and the pony had gone lame. The boy was very quiet."

Ezekiel handed over two silver coins and untied the pony from the small string of mounts. They returned with haste to The Swan, where John Croxhale explained the progress of pack ponies to Ezekiel. They carried wool bales, collected after shearing and the passage of them went along the downs, into the Hampshire and Sussex towns, sometimes maybe even as far as into Kent and so to Sandwich, to be shipped to the wool towns of Bruges and Ghent. With wool needed for weaving in England now, there was not such a huge amount going abroad, but it was still in demand by these Belgian towns.

As soon as Jenna was safely back in the Abbey, Ezekiel mounted his own horse and proceeded with as much speed as he could muster to Milborne Port with his news. There was no time to waste.

By the next day, Matthias was preparing for a journey. He was giving detailed instructions to Martin and Alice on the running of the school in his absence, for he had no idea how long he would be absent, and he could not afford to lose scholars.

Alice was heartened by the news that Luke, presuming it to have been Luke, was still alive. She determined to take on the organization of the scholars with dignity and grace, thankful that they were all supporting Matthias and herself in this terrible period. Of course, they had no idea of their mental and emotional turmoil, and Alice had now steeled herself to hide this from everyone.

Matthias planned to travel alone, feeling this would afford him speed and enable him to get as close as possible to Walter Woodman as he located the pack pony train. He knew they would use old drover tracks across the downs, but he had no idea whether they were making for Southampton or one of the smaller ports such as Chichester, Shoreham, Pevensey or even distant Sandwich. Sir Tobias cast doubts on Southampton due to its size. It was a large city with a busy port and if there was any intended dishonesty about the pack train, they would make for smaller places. Smuggling wool was a lucrative pastime; the king extracted high taxes on wool, and it was common for some pack trains to drop off bales in smaller coastal villages to be rowed out to waiting cogs, thus evading port taxes.

Davy offered to accompany Matthias, but was refused; without wishing to cause offence, Matthias remembered how badly Davy had been winded when the bogus monks had pursued them two years ago. Davy was older than Matthias, and less fit. Indeed, Matthias didn't feel particularly fit himself, despite weekly practice at the butts.

"Keep the household together, Davy. Martin and Lady Alice will be busy with the school. It falls to you to keep an eye on everything else. I have no clear idea how long it will take to catch up with this man."

"You will be armed against any robbers on the road Matthias, won't you," Alice asked, as they gathered outside Barton Holding

"With a war belt, yes, Alice. I have my sword, dagger and a small arbalest...."

"He has killed before," warned Sir Tobias. "You will need to be as cunning as he. The man Merrik tells me he is wily, skilled in weaponry and desperate to avoid capture."

Ezekiel turned up just before Matthias was ready to move off. He was armed, dressed for the journey and would brook no arguments.

"Two heads are better than one, Matthias. You may need help; I won't take no as an answer. It will be a hard ride."

So the two rode off together, Alice's eyes following them until she could see them no longer.

After they had disappeared from view, she remembered how Matthias had held her in his arms during the night after Ezekiel had returned with the information. He had been so gentle, so strong, so full of compassion for her. Their tears had mingled as they made love without their usual fierce passion but nevertheless very satisfactorily.

Luke had no idea where he was. He had never been far from his own home and the pace the man maintained was punishing. Walter Woodman was a man fuelled by the desperation of self-preservation. He had no taste for dangling at the end of a noose, his eyes picked out by crows, his entrails rotting as he hung there as a warning to his fellow miscreants. When he picked out the home of the child he had no clear plan, and his usual red rage had kicked in once he mounted the beast behind Luke.

How had he allowed his wife and son to be killed so barbarically by the damned crazed soldier...his petite common sense wife and blonde sweet faced son...he tried in his worst nightmares to reach them and failed every time, remembering only the moment of slicing cleanly across the child's neck, the grin of pleasure on the soldier's face as he held the child by his hair to wield the knife more accurately...the blood bubbling from the death wound, the child's eyes rolling in his head as the life blood streamed from him, the eyes dulled in death. A moment of inattention from himself had given the ragged, filthy soldier the opportunity to grab his son...seven years old, blonde, so mischievous that he had ventured too far into the forest while he, Walter, had searched for wood suitable for carving. By the time Walter had found him, the soldier, wounded, insanity gleaming in his glittering eyes, had seen the boy as a threat to his very life, had uttered profanities such as one wouldn't want one's child to hear and had drawn his knife, the blade gleaming in the weak sunlight streaming through the trees as he made the swift death cut. Walter had lunged helplessly at the gibbering lunatic, blood gleaming on his blade still raised in the air, an inhuman screech filling the air. Walter was never sure whether the screech had come from himself or the mad soldier, but he was sure of his next actions as he grabbed the knife from the assailant and plunged it deeply into the stomach of the man.

Moving him off the body of his son had been difficult. Shaking now with impotent rage, shock and grief, Walter staggered back through the forest to his home bearing the bloodied body of his inert son, only to find the soldier had visited his wife before finding the child, raped and killed her, leaving a scene of carnage behind him. His life had changed for ever. Angry, introverted, isolated...the red rage overtook him when he least expected it and now had landed him in desperate trouble. His mind was now as disturbed as the returning soldier's had been. Luke had almost become his own in his tortured mind, but there was no kindness or compassion remaining in his darkening soul.

The frantic plunge into the woodland behind Barton Holding had been unplanned, but exhilarating to him, guessing that this was a way rarely used being downhill towards the stream, and beset all the way by cruel twigs and branches spearing their eyes and faces. He had not stopped until they were well away from the village, and despite feeling moved by the hands of the boy holding on to him for fear of falling, he would not allow any pity to enter into his now half formed plan.

The child had seen him steal tools. His grandfather was the County Coroner - this could spell his death knell. He had stolen, killed, raped in his native town. There was a price on his head. He could not, would not kill the child. He would have to take him with him. He could be useful in some way. If he could get far enough, he might be able to find some work which was within his capability – and then, when entering the hilltop town of Shaftesbury, he had picked up the train of pack ponies.

Although not his field of work it was travelling, which suited him, especially as the animal belonging to Luke was spent and lame. He had found a tinker to take him for a coin or two, and then joined the train of pack ponies with their burden of wool bales. It would travel to Salisbury, then on to the coastal towns where there were wool bales to drop off at secret hidden coves before arriving at Sandwich, where he intended to take ship. He still had stolen silver in his well concealed purse. He trusted no-one and was ever vigilant as they trudged through the deep lanes where sheep and cattle were so often herded.

Luke watched the man uneasily. He had appeared to be deep in some reverie of his own, muttering and sweating, eyes wild and staring. Now he jerked as if pulling out of a bad dream.

"Stay where you are, brat."

Walter Woodman slouched out into the evening air, glancing round him to see the string of pack animals had stopped in a field by an inn where food could be had.

The head driver nodded to him.

"Get some food, and then you're on watch overnight," he said, giving a curt nod.

Walter took some bread and a small piece of cheese to Luke and then disappeared into the inn to find a willing slattern to give him relief before eating and settling down with the animals.

Luke was afraid of the dark, the noises of the night, the temper of Walter and of his own weakness. He had time to consider his place in Matthias' household as he walked wearily beside the pack ponies, laden as they were with bales of wool. He had never been expected to walk as far as he had on that first day, and he had cried with exhaustion long before they arrived at their destination for the first night. Walter had lashed him with his tongue as well as his hand for his whining. He had since learned not to whine. The shoes he had on his feet when he had so proudly run out of the house to show the man his pony had long disintegrated, and his clothes were dirty, stained with both vomit and urine. He wanted his mother but knew he would be ashamed for her to see him smelling as he did now. He wondered if Matthias would try and find him and then realised with a heavy heart that Matthias would not know where to start looking...they had come so far, and he, Luke, had not been fair to Matthias. He remembered Martin's words to him and was old enough to see that he should have ignored fat Titus. Oh, but it was so easy to be wise after the event.

He sat with his back resting on one of the bales of wool, staring sightlessly into the darkness. He had tried several times to ask strangers for help, but Walter was always ready to dispel any success by shouting at him to stop his lying stories and attend to his own tasks.

Luke's tasks consisted of helping to water the pack ponies, walk beside Walter and do whatever Walter told him to. The walking was hard, and even Walter couldn't understand why they were going all the way along the South coast to Sandwich when there was a reasonable chance of crossing at Southampton, but the wool train had other tasks to perform on its route, as Walter soon found out.

Smuggled wool meant the King was cheated of taxes... smuggled wool could be dropped off at various small coves and inlets along the Hampshire and Sussex coast, evading taxes, running the risk of French privateers…exciting work… dangerous liaisons.

Walter threw himself into this unexpected trade with vigour. He was adept at evading capture and always carried the stiletto he had stolen from Ezekiel's house.

Luke was left alone when a wool bale or two was detached from the panniers, the ponies being tethered near the coast, and a slimy little man whom Luke feared above all others was left on guard.

Walter always went with them sliding off into the night, first showing Luke his knife, laying it carefully across Luke's throat to indicate what he would do if Luke tried anything reckless.

By now, Luke had no energy for reckless behaviour, if indeed he could think of anything which would help himself. He became listless, unable to eat the poor food brought to him. One day he heard the wily little ferret of a look-out ask Walter why he kept Luke with him. He heard Walter's reply, explaining that he, Luke, was his son and when they arrived, they would set up a business.

Luke thought carefully about this as he listened for the return of the men. They had reached Shoreham, in Sussex, by this time and Luke had long given up any hope of returning to his home, school, friends, mother and Matthias.

He began to wonder whether this wasn't perhaps true. Was this man really his father? Maybe his mother had lied to him… what if he wasn't a knight who had fought in the French wars…what if this man really was his father? Luke was now thoroughly confused. Who was he? Where was his father? How had he come to be living so near to his grandsire and granddame…were they really his grandparents or had it all been a terrible mistake? He heard the sound of their feet on the shingled beach and knew they would be on the move by daybreak. He closed his hot, tired eyes and feigned sleep.

Matthias and Ezekiel rode fast, making the best use of the unexpected bursts of sunshine which mopped up some of the wet mud in the lanes. Matthias' mind was teeming with emotions. He had been chastened by his words to Alice, relieved at their attempt to heal the breach between them, fearful of what might have happened to Luke and most desperately worried that they may not find him alive.

They arrived in Shaftesbury in early evening and supped with the Croxhales at the Swan. After a restless night, they made for Salisbury, another hard day's ride. Nobody in Salisbury had seen or heard of any wool train passing through. There was no wool to add and even after careful enquiries in every inn or hostelry they could find, there was no expectation of any such visit.

Ezekiel and Matthias took lodgings in the Close, just inside the great gates. They knew no-one in Salisbury to speak to, but they left news at the Guildhall of a missing boy. So many children in this great city with its fine gated cathedral were poorer than Matthias had seen; Ezekiel assured him that this was as nothing compared to some other larger cities. Matthias was not sure that one missing boy from a nearby town would mean much to the reeve at the Guildhall who listened to the message.

The cathedral was majestic, its spire soaring into the grey sky, a finger pointing the way towards God.

Before they left, Matthias heard Mass in the cavernous space of the nave, praying with all his heart that they would find Luke alive; if they failed, he was uncertain that Alice would be able to bear the pain, uncertain of his own ability to sustain her.

They left the city at daybreak, leaving the graceful spire of the cathedral. Every time they looked back it was visible, surely one of the tallest in the country, Ezekiel marvelled, whilst Matthias continued to fret at the wasted time.

Southampton was an equal disappointment to them. The city was dirty, overflowing with seafaring men, some of whom swore strange oaths in guttural tongues, pushed their way through crowds with scant concern for passers-by or reeled out of ale houses to cavort with the many painted prostitutes plying their trade.

They found lodging for the night just outside the city walls, where any pack train would have to pass on their way to the harbour. Even here, beggars whined for alms, ladies of the night gathered in the narrow streets and as evening drew in, traders packed up their goods to comply with the curfew bell.

A more friendly inn keeper than they had encountered in Salisbury told them that there was no wool train expected here for several weeks, if at all. The last one had been through to the harbour side only a week since, so another was certainly not expected.

Matthias paced up and down their chamber as Ezekiel stripped to his clouts. The bed was a tolerable one, shared by just the two of them, although the room had been more expensive since the bed would have held three…Matthias had willingly paid extra for the privacy of just himself and Ezekiel. There were clean rushes on the floor, a pitcher of warm water would be theirs in the morning for washing, and a stoup of ale with some bread and honey before they left.

A chance meeting as they left their lodging the next morning put them on the right path. Ezekiel had paused to allow a small flock of sheep to pass, driven to one of the many markets by a young boy. The odour from the animals, night soil being emptied, unwashed bodies and press of people made an unwholesome smell, and both men pressed cloths to their faces as the herd passed. The lad herding the sheep laughed cheekily at them and called something over his shoulder at them as he went by.

Matthias half caught the gist of his words and caught up with him, grasping his tunic to stop him. The lad cringed away, dismayed by the expectation of a blow for cheekiness, but Matthias surprised him by asking him to repeat what he had said.

"Nothing amiss, lad…I need to hear again what you shouted to us."

The boy continued walking after the animals, but he repeated his words.

"If you want clean air and no crowds, mister, go up on the drover tracks, and the pack ponies routes. They aint for the likes of you, with your fine horses and fancy clothes, but you won't find so much stink there."

The last sentence he added when he noticed the horses, saddled and ready to mount, but Matthias didn't consider their own clothes particularly fancy compared to some of the peacock young men who paraded themselves through the streets of this city.

He studied the boy, bare feet, torn fustian tunic two sizes too big for him, a blackened eye...he fell in beside him as the sheep trotted onwards.

"Where did you get that black eye, lad? You could do with a tincture to ease the swelling."

"Nah...s'alright mister. Some braggart gave me a belt with his fist because I couldn't move the sheep quickly enough. Said I shouldn't use the pack pony trail. I was only crossing to get down here to market. He was quick with his fists."

"So you've come down from the tracks?"

"Yeah...Why d'ya wanta know?"

"I'm looking for a young boy...he may be with a train of pack ponies...we thought he'd be in this city but there's no sign of a wool consignment here."

"You wanta be really careful, mister. Some of them up there are just wool smugglers...really dangerous. I wouldn't go up there if I were you."

Matthias took a coin from his purse and handed it to the boy. His eyes shone.

"Thanks, mister...but I mean what I say...it can be dangerous, especially as you don't know the way or even where you're going."

Matthias backed away from the little herd and watched the boy go on his way, turning back to where Ezekiel was waiting for him.

"Let's go, friend," he said quietly. "We need the old tracks. Main trackways are not where we'll find our quarry."

The shepherd lad turned to watch them go as he rounded the corner, misgiving in his thoughts as he remembered the pack train he had crossed with his flock. There had been a weary child trudging doggedly along towards the end of the train, tied loosely to the end pony with rope. Perhaps he should have mentioned that. He shrugged and put the thought out of his mind as he reached his destination.

Chapter 7

Disaster on the Wool Trail

Lydia walked the children through the village to the well where she drew water to wash their clothes whilst Ennis played with Freya in the long grass opposite. She hummed to herself as she doused the garments, wringing them out when she had finished squeezing out the last remnants of the precious soap which Martin had bought for her. She gathered up her damp bundle of washing, collected her two contented girls and started for home. She had not seen Martin for some three or four days now, but she knew he must help Lady Alice in this terrible trouble. She would like to do something to help but was uncertain exactly what she could offer. Perhaps they would walk down to Barton Holding and ask Elizabeth what she could do to help.

The latest development had cast a pall over her own excitement at Martin's desire to be wed. Was it her desire as well? Yes, she truly believed it was so. Martin had been good to her, had been patient, accepted her as she was, as she had him, and now they were to be handfast at the church door – but when this horrible business was over, Martin had now said.

He had told her they could not think of it until they saw how this matter would resolve itself. If it went badly, he might be needed in Matthias' household for a little longer.

Lydia hoped it would not be long. She was not a selfish person, but she did yearn for a settled life, and truly wished for the same for Lady Alice and Master Barton.

"Things are not going well for them, are they," she remarked to Elizabeth, sitting with her in the kitchen. Elizabeth studied Lydia, her loyalty to Matthias over-riding all else.

"The loss of a child is always heart-breaking. Lady Alice is trying to be dignified in her trouble."

Lydia felt uncomfortable.

"I have spoken out of turn," she said, humbly.

Elizabeth softened a little. She understood Lydia's lack of social graces, her desire to help and support in whatever way she could.

"Why not ask Lady Alice if she would hear Ennis' letters? I hear that Martin has been teaching her, and the Lady Alice has no-one to sit with her when school is finished...."

"Oh, I couldn't do that, Elizabeth. It would be unseemly."

"Then ask Martin to request it of her. Martin and Lady Alice work together now, so Martin could ask her. Ennis would benefit from the chance, and it would help to occupy the Lady Alice."

"What would help to occupy me?" a cool voice from the door enquired.

Lydia turned quickly, distressed at being overheard, embarrassed by her forwardness.

She stumbled over her words, afraid to look into Lady Alice's face.

"Maybe you would consent to hear Ennis read while Master Barton is away...Martin has been teaching her, but he will be too busy to visit us until...until..." she tailed off, blushing hotly at her temerity.

Alice laid her hand softly on Lydia's shoulder.

"...until Master Barton's return." Alice completed the sentence for her.

Lydia raised her eyes and looked at Lady Alice.

She was pale, the shadowing under her eyes almost resembled bruising, wearing a plain working gown of dark blue, her wimple neatly arranged to conceal her hair, a woman now in tight control of herself, under huge duress and determined to remain the mistress now.

"I would be pleased to do that, Lydia. If you would allow Ennis to walk down on her own from your cottage, I will have Davy walk back with her when we are finished. In fact," Alice took a sudden risk hoping that Matthias would understand, "Why not better that offer and allow Ennis to come to us at noon time when the scholars have a break. She can sit in the class with them. There will be no need of payment."

Lydia gasped at the enormity of the offer.

"I am not "my lady", either, Lydia. Mistress Barton is a good name. When you have time, if my husband is away for several more days, we should plan your wedding feast while the men are away from home." She placed some emphasis on the word "husband" meeting Elizabeth's eyes as she did so.

Elizabeth felt a surge of relief rush through her; Mistress Alice was in command of herself once more, had controlled her fear and grief to take the reins of the school in Matthias' absence, was determined to lose no face with her household and would do her level best to ensure that Matthias lost no pupils.

"That is a very generous offer, Lydia, for Ennis," she murmured.

Lydia stammered her thanks, and Alice nodded to both women before moving through to the schoolroom again.

In truth, she had forgotten what she had come for. She had overheard the conversation as she moved into the hallway and on a whim made herself known, making the offer to Lydia without much fore thought. Now, she was pleased. Education for girls was practically non-existent, and she doubted Matthias would withdraw the offer. As she thought of Matthias, she went cold, shivering involuntarily. Her whole body felt weak, shaking with the effort of appearing to be strong. Her son was lost - the numbness crept over her as she thought of it - she would never get used to the feeling of despair and loss. What if Matthias didn't return, either? However different her new life was, she knew she must look inwards and pull out strengths she didn't know she had if she were to survive. She felt she had come a long way in just a few days.

Luke curled up, wrapping the thin blanket Walter had thrown him round his slender body. He had begun to consider whether there was any way he could help himself. Escape was impossible. He had no clear idea of where he was although he knew at the moment they were near the sea. He could hear the waves shifting the pebbles on a beach, shingle making a soothing repetitive noise as the waves broke on the deserted shore. There was a weak moon in this semi-darkness, and Luke had watched the men detach two fat wool bales from pack-ponies and stagger into the gathering darkness with them.

There were three men who were doing all the carrying, one of them was now Walter. Walter had soon picked up the essence of the work, loving the secrecy, the planning, the lure of extra money and the knowledge that he could attack and kill if he were threatened.

It had been an easy trip so far. Luke had not found it so, but the men obviously were delighted at the ease with which they had been able to march with the ponies during the day as if there was nothing wrong with their intentions, and at night, become dark blots on the landscape, dropping into coves, inlets and onto deserted beaches, watching for the flicker of a light from the sea, telling them that a boat was coming in to collect their cargo.

Smuggling was becoming big business, carrying a huge profit but also swift and terrible punishment for those caught. The King needed the taxes, the landowners needed their money and had to trust their transport but not all transport was honest, as Walter the Woodman had discovered, to his delight. He had ceased to worry about flight to the continent, - involvement in this business would be fine for him. The packhorse trails were deeply hidden from the main tracks, the men were rough, sturdy, silent, brusque and slightly sinister. That suited him. He would now seek an opportunity to rid himself of the burden of the child, - he felt he could sustain a life here with this gang of men, for a gang they were, and Walter was comfortable with his place with them after just a short time. Luke was dispensable; he would look for a chance to sell him on as a working child.

They had left the trail at Bramber, skirting the castle carefully and following a wider track through the Sussex Downs to the coast. The great castles of the South were new to Luke, who had never been further than Sherborne with its Abbey and smaller castle. He had been awed by the distant view of Arundel castle when they had stopped there for a further drop and frightened by an encounter with dogs when the gang outstayed their welcome at Bosham, near to Chichester.

He was largely ignored by the men. They had accepted that he came as part of the deal to have Walter on board, and Walter had certainly proved valuable to them. He was a canny planner, a hard worker when it served his own purpose, and quickly understood the nature of this dishonest business.

Luke shivered under the thin blanket. He saw the men leaving with their bales, heard the crunch of their feet on the shingle and tried to pick out the shape of them as they moved stealthily down the sloping beach. The tide was half out, giving a wide beach here, just to the West of Shoreham. There were not too many bales remaining for escaping taxes – a reasonable number had to remain on the ponies for the customer waiting in Sandwich to board them on his ship. The documents had to be altered to correspond with the number given to him. The leader of the pack was an educated man who had been a royal clerk before falling from grace and fleeing for his life, a desperate man engaged in desperate activities, which nevertheless thrilled them all to their rotten cores. Walter had truly joined their ranks.

Luke was startled to hear shouting from the beach. These operations normally took place in silence. He raised himself on an elbow and peered into the gloom. Suddenly his mouth was stopped by a dirty hand clamped firmly over it. The slimy little lookout hissed into his ear.

"Trouble on the beach. Don't even think of calling out or I'll slit your scrawny little throat."

The man's cruel hands bit into Luke's shoulders, holding him hard, sitting up himself to see better what trouble they had encountered.

There was the sudden click of an arbalest releasing its catch, the cruel quarrel speeding through the air - more shouts - the little man slid backwards from Luke, clambered to his feet and took off as fast as he was able, leaving Luke alone.

As the slimy one ran, he was targeted on the top of the rise at the edge of the beach. Luke watched in horror as he fell backward and toppled to his death as the arbalest fired a second time.

Now grunts and cries of wounded men could be heard and more shouting. The smugglers had been ambushed.

In a blind panic, Luke scrambled backwards towards the rough scrub edging the narrow track down which they had travelled, clambering over the body of the slimy lookout, blood coming from his nose and mouth and still twitching in his death throes. The ponies, just two of them, had eyes rolling with panic, backing, attempting to rear, snorting with fear.

Luke laid a hand on the back of one of them for comfort – he snickered softly to the beast, hardly aware of what he was doing, so shocked was he. The pack ponies were not very much bigger than Luke, but they could not be calmed...they continued to rear and prance. He had no idea which way to run nor what was happening. He could now hear the hiss of metal on metal; they were using swords, daggers - two men locked in deadly combat crawled up the beach towards him, panting and gasping. Luke saw that one was Walter the Woodman, blood streaming from a near death cut across his stomach. Before the child's horrified eyes, blood was soaking fast into his tunic as he crawled towards Luke, thrusting with his dagger at his assailant. The assailant was a stranger; his face was cut, blood running down his face, and one arm at a useless angle, broken, would need a bone setter before he could use it again.

The world appeared to pass in front of Luke's eyes in slow motion. Walter's red rage was up. Despite his deadly wound, he was slashing and slashing over and over with the stiletto he had stolen from Ezekiel's house which Luke recognized with terror. How had Ezekiel's knife appeared there? Was Ezekiel on the beach? Had his friend's father become involved in this nightmare he found himself in? The ambush was over quickly; Luke was unable to turn his eyes away as Walter raised his dagger arm and with his last spurt of strength slid Ezekiel's stiletto deep into the throat of his assailant.

Silence had fallen on the beach; the only sound was the shuddering, rasping sound coming from Walter the Woodman who was now inching ever closer to Luke. Luke was paralysed with fear. As Walter's blood-stained hand gripped Luke's arm, a grip from which there was no escaping, Luke felt the slippery warmth of the fast flowing blood and losing control of his bladder, closed his eyes with shame. Walter was beyond noticing, beyond much at all. The slash he had received across his stomach was deep, beyond repair but he was not in his death throes just yet.

The slimy little man who had fled lay just beyond help, the arbalest had done its work.

"Get up, brat. Look to see who is left. Go down the beach." Walter's voice was thin, ragged, gasping between each forced word. Luke prised the bloody hand from his arm with difficulty. Walter was unaware of how tightly he had gripped Luke, feeling beginning to leave him.

There was a strange rattle in his throat, Luke noticed, as he spoke.

The beach in the moonlight on that late Summer night was something which would never leave Luke all his life. It was his first taste of man killing man, of deadly wounds to the death, of the power of weapons.

The wet sand was spoiled with blood mingling with the rivulets of the incoming tide turning the shore into coloured marble. The beach sloped down steeply here, shingle banks making walking difficult. Luke slid down the shifting shingle grazing his legs and fell onto a youth who had not been part of the wool train. He was dead, an arrow straight through his chest, pinning him to the damp sand beneath him. His nose and mouth were a mess of congealed blood. Luke looked away quickly and swallowed the bile rising in his throat. His urge to vomit was unbearably strong. He counted two more bodies, and found one more lying in the lapping water at the edge of the sea, staining the sea with blood. Luke recognized this man, although of the leader there was no sign, but as he stared desperately at the scene, the child noticed a light bobbing on the water some way out and could hear the splash of oars. With a wisdom beyond his six years, he guessed the leader had fled with the boat and the wool bales.

Luke climbed back up the shingle shelf to where he had left Walter, now lying with glazed eyes, the rattle in his throat more marked.

"All dead."

There was no answer from Walter; Luke sat on the ground beside his dying captor, cross legged, waiting patiently for he knew not what, tears coursing down his grimy face.

Matthias and Ezekiel found the packhorse trail more difficult to travel at speed. The rains of this wet Summer had submerged parts in muddy water, and it was not long before the horses were splashed with dirt. It was silent on this path through the downs above Southampton, leading into the chalklands of Hampshire and Sussex. In places the trail was deep between high hedges, making everything seem dark and cut off from the world. They encountered no-one during the first couple of hours riding, and had little to say to one another, often striving to keep their mounts steady. They noticed evidence of previous users, however. There were obvious places where travellers had stopped - horse dung, remnants of fires, an occasional discarded item.

Matthias was quick to understand that any discarded thing might be from Luke if he had travelled that way, so items were examined carefully, however old or wet or insignificant they appeared, but there was nothing.

It was windy in these hills, the wind funnelling through the sheltered trails. Twice Matthias stopped his horse and looked back along the trail.

"I think we are being followed, Ezekiel."

"Who on earth would know us in these parts?"

"You're probably right...it must be the wind crawling through these tunnelled passages"

They continued to battle on through the inhospitable landscape, but even as they went, Matthias' feeling of being followed increased. He remembered all too clearly the uncanny feeling he had experienced as they rode through the gates of Paris when he had seen the body of the unnamed courtesan. It was the same feeling.

They stopped at Hog's Lodge, near an ancient Roman encampment, a mass of high hills providing a slightly sinister backdrop. Angry thunder clouds threatened rain, and the wind continued to rise. The only shelter was a clump of trees at the base of the rising ground, and the two men tethered their horses and made use of a roughly constructed bothy, conveniently meant for shelter whilst on the trail. It was dank and musty, clearly not having been used overmuch recently. Matthias undid his pack to share a cold pie with Ezekiel, who produced two apples he had picked up before leaving the bustle of Southampton's markets.

They had been riding all day, had covered some fifteen miles and were tired, saddle-sore and Matthias found himself to be jumpy, constantly on the watch for signs of being followed. Ezekiel could not understand his feelings and said as much. Matthias was unable to explain it, but just as darkness fell, they heard the unmistakable sound of hooves thudding on the rough turf of the track.

The rhythm of the beats indicated a gallop, and as the bothy was slightly off the track, and the horses were tethered behind the ramshackle construction, Matthias indicated to Ezekiel that they should remain silent and still, watching through the fading light to see who followed them.

Although it was hard to make out features, there were two horsemen who did not stop at the bothy but rode straight on, clearly in a hurry. Their galloping pace seemed to show that they were regular users of the trackway, and the pace gave away the urgency of their journey.

"If they were in that much of a hurry you would think they should be using the regular tracks rather than these pack trails," Ezekiel commented.

Matthias was more perceptive. "They were after something- or someone; they were very sure of the way. They seemed not to mind riding these paths after dark."

Wrapped in their heavy cloaks, they settled down for several hours of uncomfortable sleep, waking as the dawn broke, chilled and stiff from their inhospitable lodging.

Mounting to begin a second day's ride with still no clue as to whether they were on the right trail, Matthias looked back over the way they had travelled the day before. The downs were translucent in this early dawn light, all trace of the thunder clouds and the wind gone. Birdsong brightened the morning and a dew pond nearby, a feature of these downs in some places, glistened in the beams of the sun as it rose. The early shaft of sunlight also picked out a figure trudging towards them. At first Matthias thought it could be Luke, but that was quite irrational, he realised as he saw with surprise that it was the shepherd lad he had spoken to in Southampton, bigger than Luke, probably about ten or eleven Summers.

As he drew near he waved, indicating that he wanted to speak with them. Matthias walked his horse back down the track towards the lad.

"Is it a ride you're after?" Matthias asked him, noticing his bare feet.

"You shouldn't be up here," the boy began, ignoring the offer.

"There's two men who saw you take the trail. They were in the market and I overheard them. "

"Why should that bother us?" Matthias wondered,

"They think you are King's tax men. The last pack ponies were part of their smuggling ring. I told you it was dangerous. They mean to catch up with you and kill you."

"I think they overtook us last evening," began Matthias, but the boy tugged urgently at his reins.

"Listen will you - there's a gang who work up here - they had a young boy tied with a piece of rope to one of the ponies. I should have told you that before."

The words tumbled out of him. He was thinking of the despairing walk, the weariness, the beaten, bewildered look - how would it be if these gentlemen were really looking for a lost son from a high born family - might he be rewarded with a bit of silver? What could he do with a bit of luck! He would like some shoes, for one thing, and maybe a hot pie or two.

Matthias leant down from his saddle and hoisted the lad up in front of him.

"That's a very big horse, mister...." His face was full of awe.

"Tell me about these men." Matthias turned his horse and walked it back to where Ezekiel was waiting.

"There were two of them. I seen 'em before, so I knew they were part of the gang. Everyone in Southampton knows them. They can do what they like. I told you it was too dangerous up here...they seen you make for the trails."

"Did you walk all the way to catch up with us?" Ezekiel asked him, pulling his horse round to walk side by side with Matthias so he could hear.

"I got a lift a bit of the way with me da - he's got a cart with an old nag - he carts dung and stuff - then I walked - I'm used to these trails and I reckoned you'd maybe stop for the night."

"Tell me about the child," Matthias ordered.

"He was younger than me, maybe about six Summers, quite small, a bit of rope round his middle tied to the last pack pony. He looked tired."

"Hair colour?"

But the lad couldn't say.

"What was he wearing?" he couldn't tell them that, either, but he did know where they were making for - a piece of information his da had told him.

"What's left of their wool ends up in Sandwich me da says. They might drop off at Bosham, Shoreham, Pevensey, and then straight on to Sandwich."

"You're very knowledgeable about these men," Ezekiel said, wondering where all this inside information came from.

"Me da's been with them once or twice. He doesn't do it anymore since he saw them kill a watchman in Bosham. He keeps well out of their way. Keeps his mouth shut, too, mostly."

Matthias was disturbed at the matter of fact way the youth issued the information but nevertheless made a decision.

"You can either come with us – you'll have to ride with one of us - it will be uncomfortable, but we can manage - or you can turn and go back. We need to press on. We're now behind these two men, so we will travel as fast as we can."

The boy's eyes lit up. "Can I come with you, mister? I won't be any trouble, and I might be able to help. I've been down this coast a bit, so I know Bosham and I know Shoreham. Never been to Pevensey or Sandwich."

Matthias and Ezekiel exchanged a nod.

"Let's be on our way then," Matthias said, settling the lad more securely in front of him.

"Hold on to the saddle horn and tell us your name."

"I'm Ralph, will we go fast, mister?"

"As fast as we can. You tell me if you feel unsafe...you'll soon get into the rhythm."

"A tip, mister - we're at least a day and a half behind them - don't bother with Bosham - make for Shoreham."

With those young words of wisdom ringing in his ears, Matthias decided that was now where they were headed.

Chapter 8

Pursuit Continues

Merrik hung around in Sherborne for several more days after the fair had moved on. He wanted to be near to the source of information concerning Walter the Woodman, and he guessed Sir Tobias would be around Sherborne, and willing to share information with him.

He did not feel equipped or able to go after the man himself, having no horse and being an itinerant player, albeit one who had just refused to accompany the rest of the troupe to their next fair.

He wandered into the Abbey several times, gazing up at the soaring roof, listening to the muted sound of the monks as they sang their offices, enjoying watching Edric work on his carving.

The carving fascinated and calmed him. It was imaginative, skilled work, designed in part by Robert Hull, the overall architect who worked from Exeter. He allowed the craftsmen working in the Abbey a certain leeway, according to their expertise, and Edric exploited this in his carvings. He was not a talkative man, but his apprentice, Peterkin, was.

From him Merrik learned of the sudden attack on Peterkin and Walter's swift flight. Merrik knew that Walter was adept at both flight and concealment and was convinced that they might find some of the stolen items of value if they could learn where Walter had been living. He began by looking around the tenements on the outskirts of the town, tucked behind wealthier houses.

Sherborne was a small town, rich in tall buildings owned by the wealthier citizens, some still constructed of mud and wattle with much use of local oak to reinforce; any stone used was often of a soft, mellow colour, windows glassed with tiny panes, second level overhanging the rough pavements. Some of the lanes were scarcely wide enough for a horse and rider, but most had a leat or drain running down the middle to catch the night-time slops flung out of upper windows.

Behind these grand houses were smaller dirtier alleys where the dwellings were shabbier, less secure, often crumbling and in need of constant repair. Here, families lived in one room and slept together, using a common privy on the scrubby land at the rear of the rows of dwellings. Animals wandered among the weeds, a pig, several fowl, feral cats, a couple of threatening looking dogs.

In between his frequent visits to the Abbey, Merrik searched these alleys, guessing that it would have been in a place such as this that Walter found shelter.

He swung between a flurry of activity, searching outbuildings, asking questions and then moods of depression, remembering his brother, considering the fate of his sister. She could not have been involved in any killing, she was an innocent, pretty and naïve. He hoped they would find Walter the Woodman and bring him back to face justice, or she would hang.

Sherborne folk were watchful of strangers; after two or three days it had been noticed that Merrik was searching for something and had not moved on with the players. He was asked bluntly whether he was up to no good; what was he doing, who did he expect to find?

Drinking in an ale house that evening, Merrik found it easy to loosen his tongue and explain what he was seeking and why. Townsfolk were interested, supportive and sympathetic. They also knew of people who had experienced theft of clothing, food, silver over the last few weeks.

"There's several deserted places near the Abbey's mill, at the back of Acreman Street," Walter Gallor advised him. "They haven't been used for years...crumbling...beaten by wind and rain, but might be good for a few nights shelter."

Merrik ventured out there the next morning. The collection of ruins were only half standing, walls crumbling after enduring rain, wind, snow and whatever other ravages time threw at them. A couple were still half roofed, doors leaning crazily adrift, rubble and weeds belying the suggestion that once this had been a happy little enclave of people before they were smitten with the black death nearly a hundred years ago and had died or fled.

The better of the two roofed ones had evidence of recent occupation, and Merrik sat down heavily on the damp ground, sad eyes examining the place where surely Walter the Woodman had hidden and sheltered. There were no comforts in the place. Surely all those years ago a family had taken their scant belongings and fled the raging plague as it spread from Weymouth, respecting no-one.

Ashes of a fire were scuffed in the doorway, or where the doorway should have been. Walter had obviously used the back of the place as a midden leaving a gut-wrenching smell of human waste.

A dirty and torn pair of hose had been trodden into the earth floor, and lifting these from the earth packed floor, Merrik cast his eyes onto a fallen timber, a silver candlestick poking up behind it at a drunken angle. He moved the timber and looked down at Walter's hoard of stolen items. Small things he had taken with him, but these larger items which he had clearly thought to sell for silver whenever he could, had been left behind.

So this dingy place was where Walter had hidden himself. Merrik smiled grimly to himself; he would bring the bailiff to see Walter's hoard; if he returned, he would most certainly face serious charges for theft, even a hanging. But Merrik would prefer Walter to hang for murder and rape...the theft was minor compared to that.

Alice had counted eight days now since Matthias had ridden away. This was the ninth. She made sure that her lessons were well prepared; she could not bear the shame if she caused Matthias to lose scholars during his absence, and she was careful to speak to families who called to collect their boys, to reassure them that she was grateful for their support. All families were at the moment giving comfort to Alice, relieving Davy of the task of escorting the boys to the village so that he could assist Alice with chores outside school time. It occurred to Alice that it was more likely they were anxious that their own boys should not be abducted, as without Luke or Matthias at home, the household tasks were much lightened. There was a certain fear emanating around the place, not knowing whether the abduction was perhaps marauding soldiers returning from France or even political snatching for armies, for the unrest in the country was beginning to spread gradually, like some ungainly spillage.

She found sleep hard. As soon as her head touched the feather pillow, her mind began to teem with frightful imaginings. The curtains round the tester bed gave her a false feeling of security when she first lay down, but once she had extinguished the candle, images of Luke and Matthias flickered before her eyes. Every sound outside was magnified; if an owl hooted she thought it might be a signal from some wolfshead; if the timbers of the house creaked, then it must be footsteps. Each night she was still tossing and turning as the dawn chorus began, and her stale mind fought to appear calm and strong as the day progressed.

Elizabeth, Davy and Martin tried not to let her see that they were watching her like hawks, fearful for her state of mind. William called over each day with messages from Sir Tobias and Lady Bridget. Alice had implored them to remain in their own home and allow her to make progress with Matthias' work, and mindful of the feeling that she had been too indulged by them, they wisely agreed. It was time for Alice to grow on her own, however hard this might appear.

Martin stayed in the schoolroom each day with Alice after the boys had left, preparing the lessons for the next day. Although lettered, Martin needed guidance and help to deliver when he was on his own. Alice had taken the older boys, the ones Matthias was nurturing, and Martin had taken Alice's place in the little room. Although Martin enjoyed the work, he found it quite a strain, for he did not move well. He quickly devised a way of giving individual help to each boy by them coming to him rather than he walking around, correcting as he went, - Alice's preferred method. He was aware of the strain on his good eye, too. The ointment given to him by Ezekiel was long finished.

On the tenth afternoon Titus' father requested an audience with Alice.

She dreaded what he was going to say, fearing this might be the beginning of a defection of scholars. She was not wrong.

"How long is this going to go on?" he demanded, starting bullishly.

"I cannot give an answer to that," Alice replied.

"Surely some reduction in fees is in order?"

"Do you have some complaint regarding my work, Sir?"

The direct question floored Master Fuller for a moment.

"Well...no, but we did not expect our sons to be taught by a woman."

So that was the nub of it, Alice thought.

"I did not expect my son to be abducted," she countered.

"I understood from my son that he has run away. It seems that he has done this before."

The unfairness of the remark caught Alice between the shoulder blades and she almost gasped audibly before countering swiftly without considering any options.

"Had Titus not behaved in such an unmannerly way towards me, my son would not have felt the unhappiness which caused him to run away - once only."

Titus' father was clearly taken aback.

"Titus is not an unmannerly boy, Mistress Barton. What proof do you have that he has behaved so?"

Alice was relieved that Matthias had thought to share Martin's story of Titus with her, and emboldened by this knowledge, she had no hesitation in explaining the events to him.

Her words caused Master Fuller's face to redden with embarrassment as she revealed the entire story to him.

"I wish Master Barton had told me of this," he said unhappily. "I would have dealt with my son. This is shameful."

"Titus begged my husband not to speak to you, and he was offered a second chance. There is little merit in chastising him now. All the scholars are desperate to have Luke returned safely."

Alice heard the wobble in her voice as she uttered the last words, and Master Fuller bowed stiffly to her in recognition of her loss.

"Allow me to withdraw my remarks, Mistress Barton. I will do my best to keep all families on your side until Master Barton returns."

After he had left Alice found herself shaking. She had stood her ground with some success, but it did sound as if Master Fuller had come as the elected spokesperson.

What was Matthias doing right now, she wondered. Had they picked up any trace of her son?

She hoped she had done right in speaking out with Master Fuller. It had been too personal for her taste, but she had done what she thought best. She hoped and prayed it did not backfire on her.

Luke crawled away from the dying man, shaking, sobbing, bruising his knees on the rough ground. As he reached the top of the shingle stack he looked back to see that Walter had ceased moving, and he could no longer hear the dreadful death rattle.

There had been three men assigned to this rendezvous on the beach, - one, the leader, had escaped with the incoming boat, another was dead on the fore shore, and now Walter, too, was gone. The child was alone but for the two pack ponies they had brought with them to carry the bales.

Painfully he rose to his feet, wondering what he should do. He had seen Walter use the stiletto which he had once seen in Ezekiel's house, but he had caught no sign of Ezekiel on the beach. In his confused mind, he felt he should rescue the dagger and keep it with him. He slid down the shingle on his bottom and tentatively released the dagger from Walter's clasped and bloodied hand, closing his eyes as he did so to avoid having to look at the copious blood flowing still from the death wound.

His strength was exhausted when he reached the comparative safety of the ponies, still hobbled on the scrubby grass edging the approach to this deserted beach. He wondered where the attackers had come from - were they good people or were they a rival gang? He had no idea, and he didn't really care at that moment.

Suddenly Luke felt older and wiser and began to think for himself. He remembered the stories Matthias had told of the exploits of Alexander the Great, thought of Martin and how he had struggled home from France, badly wounded. He himself was not wounded - he had simply watched others and discovered the harsh realities of life outside his own comfortable existence. What might Matthias do in his position? Was anyone looking for him? Did his Mother think he had died? All these thoughts crossed his mind as he leaned wearily against one of the pack ponies, taking a little warmth from its body.

He had lingered too long. He may have felt wiser, but his six-year old self had not reckoned with the quick wits and ready actions of the remaining members of the gang who were guarding the remains of the consignment. One of the men swiftly scooped up the ponies, dragging Luke with them, to re-join the rest, stumbling hastily up the tracks back to the waiting party.

Luke found himself once more tied roughly to the last pony, and the gang hastened onwards, anxious to put distance between themselves and the disaster that was Shoreham.

There was one difference, however. Luke was now more aware of his perilous situation; he had enjoyed some sort of ragged protection whilst Walter the Woodman was alive. He didn't understand why, but now Walter was dead he knew his days with this group of men were numbered. As they plodded onwards, Luke caught snatches of their conversation, and understood that when they reached their final destination he would be cast aside, dead or alive, with no protection. There was talk of selling him to the captain of the cog which would carry the remainder of the wool to the continent - argument about the wisdom of this course of action and who would carry out the task rumbled on until Luke started to lose his new sense of purpose and was very afraid.

They stopped for a few hours rest at a broken- down shack near the Devil's Dyke, a high spot on the Sussex downs, gloomy and mysterious. The sojourn in the shack was short lived. They had been there but a short while when two riders caught up with them. Luke was huddled in a corner trying to appear disinterested as they spoke with the remainder of the gang.

It seemed that their main worry was Luke himself, as they had observed two riders, armed and well equipped, joining the track. At first they thought these men were King's men, pursuing the gang for tax evasion and smuggling but they had also been overheard asking questions about the trail, had mentioned a missing child and so it was imperative that these strangers were located and dealt with.

Luke thought desperately as to how he could escape their gaze, but to no avail. He was picked up bodily by one of the men, none too gently, and found himself slung onto the front of the saddle of the younger man who mounted behind him.

The horses were kicked into action and they were off, pounding along the trail leaving the slower train of pack ponies and their diminishing load well behind.

Matthias and Ezekiel under the guidance of their new-found friend reached Shoreham shortly after Luke had left. Ralph knew where the men would have met the boat and took them away from the drover roads and down towards the beach.

Dawn had broken, and at first as they stood at the top of the shingle bank, Matthias thought what a peaceful scene was before his eyes, the tide now incoming, the sea breaking on the pebbly shore and the light from the sky turning the horizon a pleasing rosy pink.

However, as soon as they moved down towards the water, they saw a very different picture.

Walter's body lay contorted, blood congealed, staining the stones upon which he lay. A little further down the shore was another body, and looking to his right, Matthias noticed a body fixed almost to the ground by an arrow which had penetrated his neck at great force.

Ezekiel crouched down and felt for a pulse; there was none, but he confirmed that this was the man whose tooth he had pulled. Overcoming his revulsion, Matthias turned him over to search for any evidence which might assist them and was about to turn away to examine the other bodies when he noticed the ribbon tied round the man's wrist. It was the ribbon which Luke had tied on the mane of his pony when he first rode him, and which the man had kept lest he was able to claim him back from the tinker in Shaftesbury. It had been his proof of ownership as agreed with the tinker. Matthias untied this carefully and put it in his pouch.

He was suddenly afraid that this might be where Luke, too had met his death, and with trembling in all his limbs he searched the beach feverishly, striding a little way into the water past the body lying there, gently moving in the rippling sea water. Ezekiel watched him with dread. Finally Matthias was convinced that there was no small body lying on this deserted shore.

"I don't know what has happened here, but there is no sign of Luke, although he may have been here."

Ralph was anxious to leave the scene before any bailiff or other source of authority should discover the carnage.

"Mister…we don't want to be found here. We'll be apprehended as culprits - let's be on our way."

The two men saw the sense of this, and they hastened off the beach, moving back onto the tracks the wool train would have followed.

Matthias was now frantic with concern that Luke should have been exposed to such a scene. The death wound which Walter Woodman had received was a mess of blood and exposure of entrails. Luke had been a protected child, loved and nurtured, unused to such violence. It was imperative to find him, restore him to his own people, if there was still time to do this.

Ralph was a more hardened lad; he had seen the gangs in action; he left them in no doubt about their violence. He had seen and heard about other deaths, fights, beheadings, abductions. The smuggling was big business with healthy profits, and the men at the head of these gangs were vicious and ruthless.

Ralph's advice now was to press on to Sandwich with all due speed.

However, Matthias was unwilling to continue with Ralph as a passenger; it had slowed them up a little, and he was now desperate to catch up with whoever was now holding Luke before they dispatched him completely. The only solution he could think of was for Ezekiel to return to Southampton and wait, taking Ralph with him. He would then abandon these heavy- going pack ways and find a faster route through, - the track honest merchants and pilgrims would use. As long as he could reach Sandwich before Luke was bundled onto a cog or killed by the gang - that was the most important thing.

Reluctantly, Ezekiel agreed. Ralph was overcome with remorse, feeling he had slowed them down, but Matthias reassured the lad that without his guidance, they would not have thought to leave the downs and go lower down to Shoreham. If they had missed Shoreham they would not have seen Walter and known of his death, nor seen the ribbon round Walter's wrist.

"How many days have we been on this quest?" Ezekiel muttered, as they sorted their packs out before separating.

"We have been away for nearly nineteen days now, by my reckoning," Matthias told him, as he divided the weapons between them, ensuring that both men were well protected.

His eyes felt hot and gritty, he was dirty, stinking of sweat and horse, hungry for a hot meal and more fearful of the outcome of their journey than he would have liked.

"Wait for me in the same inn we used before," Matthias told him, "but if there is no sign of me within five days, make for home. Do you have sufficient coin?"

Ezekiel assure him that he did, and the two friends parted with heavy hearts.

Chapter 9

Ezekiel Returns

Alice had cause to be grateful to Master Fuller, for after nearly three weeks of absence there was little feeling of disquiet among the parents of the scholars. Alice had ensured that all lessons were scrupulously prepared, that Martin's work was overseen by herself and that the days were exactly as they would have been if Matthias himself had been there. Master Fuller made his satisfaction with the current arrangements very vocal, encouraging everyone to support the school, for, he argued, where else would they send their boys?

Ennis was thrilled to be permitted to sit in on the afternoon lessons and drank in all the information eagerly. The boys ignored her for the most part, but were not unkind - they just took no notice of her.

Alice hoped that when - sometimes she found herself thinking if - Matthias returned, he would agree to Ennis continuing, for she was certainly not slow and loved the experience.

Elizabeth and Davy were becoming very fearful for Matthias as the days went on - the three weeks seemed long, and they had no means of knowing where he was.

Sir Tobias gave up all pretence of staying away to help Alice grow and adjust, and after another full week had passed, he rode in with William, insisting that Alice should dine with them on Sunday, after Mass. Alice agreed, but after a few hours, she left, needing to be at home lest any sudden news should come.

Lady Bridget was pleased with her daughter's new resolve. She perceived an awakening in Alice of a sense of responsibility which she had not shown before. Some of Matthias' burden would now be on Alice's shoulders, and that pleased her mother.

Sir Tobias had news for them of Merrik and his finding of the stolen goods; he also felt it only right that Alice should know why the man Walter was fleeing - what crimes he had committed, and how Merrik was so convinced that Walter would not harm Luke.

Sir Tobias was not so sure, but he kept his thoughts to himself.

As Justice of the Peace, he had duties which took him away from home more frequently, and he attempted to discover more about Merrik's sister, but Bradford by Avon was in a neighbouring county, and too far for Sir Tobias to have any influence. He knew she would have to face the heavy consequences of associating too closely with Walter. That was the law, harsh though it sometimes seemed.

Davy had been escorting Ezekiel's sons home at the end of the afternoon. It made Davy's days very long, but he was pleased to be able to do something to help. The boys were very subdued with Ezekiel away and Martha was finding it difficult to keep their spirits up.

Alice arranged a treat for Martha and the boys one Sunday afternoon; Davy rode over to escort them; Martha had packed a repast for the boys and herself, leaving their maid to enjoy some free time.

The late Summer was on the point of becoming early Autumn. The wretched state of the wet ground had given yet another poor harvest, and food would be scarce and expensive this coming Winter. Alice and Elizabeth had looked on the bushes and hedgerows around them and noted that although there were blackberries, they were small and would be ruined in the next heavy rainfall, so they should be gathered for the treat of a tasty pastry; likewise the hips and sloes glowing on the bushes would not last. The berries were needed for cordials against coughs, together with honey from the bees - not so rich this year either.

Alice ached for the absence of Matthias and Luke to join this attempt at a pleasant afternoon to lift all their spirits. She had invited Martin to join them with Lydia and the girls, so together with Elizabeth and Davy, they were a noisy party with a forced sense of gaiety.

The best fruits were in the hedgerows leading to the lane which led directly into Milborne Port itself, and the party spread themselves out, industriously picking, calling to the children and looking back at Martin, who sat on an upturned cask, guarding the pots of picked fruit and their feast.

Martin was tired; he had stretched himself day after day to support Alice, and with no ointment left now for his eyes, he suffered with continuous eye strain as well as aching limbs from needing to move around in his work with the scholars. He had seen little of Lydia in these two weeks, and he missed that sorely. She was picking with Ennis and keeping an eye on Freya, playing in the mud on the path.

He hoped Matthias was safe. He knew from experience how dangerous the tracks could be, especially in unfamiliar territory.

Alice had attempted to talk to him about planning his forthcoming nuptials, but he had no enthusiasm for planning at present – let Matthias be home and safe first, he had told her, and she had given up.

There was sun that afternoon, so they gathered round Martin and spread out across the path to enjoy freshly baked bread, soft cheese, and some marchpane, sent by Lady Bridget.

They were packing up when they heard hoofbeats; Lydia snatched Freya up and held her close, her muddy hands marking Lydia's simple dress. Martin reached for his crutches and moved out of the path as the horse came into sight.

It was a solemn sight, no strident galloping, - just a steady plod. Martha scrunched her eyes and shielded them with her hand.

"It's Ezekiel!" Her cry was heartfelt, but Alice's heart dropped; he was alone, and clearly weary. Davy moved closer to her, Martin also struggling to get his balance to protect her.

"A party! When I've just ridden a ten-day journey! My word!" but he was attempting a jest, and as Alice's eyes met his she dreaded the story behind the journey.

"We've been gathering berries - our days have been long with no news," she faltered, breathless with fear.

"I have news. Let's go in." His tone was sombre, his eyes sad, his face strained.

He dismounted and hugged Martha tight, his boys waiting patiently behind their mother for their turn.

"Lydia, can you take the children into the schoolroom and look after them while Master Jacobson tells his news," Alice asked.

It was a serious party with bated breath which crowded into the solar, anxious to hear Ezekiel's words.

Alice dreaded what she might hear, but she was certain he would not have gathered them all together if the news had been of death. He would have told her alone.

"First, when I left, Matthias was alive; we have traced Luke and at that point we believe he too was still alive, but in deadly peril."

The silence in the solar was utter. Alice felt her fingernails digging remorselessly into the palms of her hand. Martin instinctively put his hand on her shoulder for comfort, and she did not remove it.

Ezekiel began the story from where they had picked up the trace of the pony in Shaftesbury. He could not tell them how Luke arrived in Shaftesbury, except that it would have been by pony, presumably with his abductor, whom they guessed to have been Walter the Woodman.

He was a faithful story teller – they were with him every step of the way...unfriendly Salisbury, more welcoming Southampton...a waste of time in both places had they known better...the boy Ralph, who Ezekiel had left in Southampton suitably rewarded...their uncomfortable ride along the pack trails...finding evidence of carnage in Shoreham - not a place where they would have thought of going had it not been for Ralph. Evidence of gang warfare on the beach at Shoreham was bloody and gruesome. As she heard the details of Walter's death, Alice felt her throat go dry, her eyes became unfocused. Her head swam. Martin tightened his grip on her shoulder, taking one of her hands. They were deadly cold.

"Smuggling is very big business," Ezekiel told them. Martha was ashen faced, Elizabeth leaned on Davy, her hands covering her face to prevent Alice glimpsing the horror she felt.

"We guessed Luke would have been found by the two men who were looking for us - they must be something high in the organization. With Walter dead, it seems obvious that these men, high born by the cut of their clothes and the quality of their horses, would wish to silence Luke in some way. The boy Ralph suggested it might be worth their while to sell him to a sea captain as a cabin boy, and therefore they might be making for Sandwich. That is where what remains of the wool bales is destined."

"Where is Sandwich?" Alice asked, her voice coming from far away in her own head.

"Kent, a county of much disorder in past years and probably still pretty lawless," Ezekiel told her.

"Many days ride then," Martin commented.

"Indeed. Our silver was running low and our horses were spent. Matthias decided he should make for Sandwich with all due speed, and the presence of Ralph was slowing us down. He asked me to return to Southampton, see Ralph safely delivered there, and wait five days for him. If he had not returned there by the end of five days, I was to return home to tell of the progress."

"There was no way of getting messages to us?"

"No – we do not have the liberty to use royal messengers – even if one should be travelling in this direction, which seems a rarity."

An uneasy silence fell in the solar.

"So – we wait still," Alice said, attempting to make her voice strong and resolute.

"Yes. There is nothing else we can do – except pray," Ezekiel agreed.

Luke was now terrified and sick with fear at the pace they were travelling and could only hold on tightly to the saddle horn of the great horse on which he found himself. The men did not speak as they rode, crouched low mostly galloping, occasionally slowing to a canter. Once they stopped at an ale house high above the coast. The two men shared the bed and Luke was thrown a blanket and curled up on the floor, too miserable to move. He slept a little before being roughly woken and bundled back onto the horse of the second rider.

There had been a snatch of conversation between the two men as they prepared for sleep, and Luke tried to listen and understand, but it was hard; he heard mention of a cog bound for Calais; he heard Ghent mentioned but he had no idea what or where that was. He understood that he was worth money to them rather than kill him - they were talking about the captain of the cog and delivering Luke to him. He allowed himself to cry a little, remembering the warmth and safety of his mother's arms and then recalling stories of the bravery of Matthias and Martin - was there any way he could help himself? He tried not to think about the terrible scene on the beach, but when he closed his eyes he found he was re-living the moment of seeing Walter's death wound - so much blood.

He tried to imagine himself back in the safety of the school room. He enjoyed Matthias' stories; he tried hard at his studies and had friends amongst the scholars, - yes – even Titus. He found himself hoping that if he didn't ever see his mother again that Matthias would comfort her and would do whatever people had to do to give his mother another child to love. Titus had not told him how it happened - only that he would be neglected if another baby came. He didn't think

Titus was correct in that. Now he was so far away, he could think about this more clearly and he was certain his adored mother loved him.

Matthias was grateful for his father's insistence that he should be a competent horseman as a youngster, for now he rode fast and furiously. If he reached Sandwich too late, Luke would be gone, and how then to retrieve him?

Now using a more regular route, the going was easier, and he found himself needing to stop after a hard day of riding. Although reluctant to pause, he was wise enough to recognize that both he and his mount could not be expected to travel at that speed without some rest. There was a Cluniac Abbey in Lewes, and Matthias was glad to avail himself of their hospitality to travellers. He found the peace of the monks calming and was more than grateful for the simple food and clean bedding, especially for the ministrations of their ostler, who rubbed his horse down well and provided food.

Although he enquired of the gatekeeper, it appeared that the two men, who would have had the young Luke with them, had not stopped in Lewes.

Matthias hoped they had stopped somewhere - he did not think they would be able to travel the distance without breaking their journey, for Sandwich was still many miles away. He wondered why they needed to travel so far, and as he reflected, he came to the conclusion that the gang had a chain of corrupt officials, sea going vessels, gang members, which dictated to which ports they must travel.

In his safe world of Milborne Port and Sherborne, this violence and corruption was a shock to him which he found difficult to comprehend.

The weather was showing signs of deteriorating as he rode the next day. A cold wind whistled through his cloak, despite it still being only September. Sweat dried on his body uncomfortably as he rode, sometimes failing to go as fast as he wanted due to other travellers on the road. At one point a royal messenger scattered all before him as he tore through the crowded fairway. Matthias attempted to put some distance between himself and the other travellers to increase his speed.

Storm clouds were gathering out at sea, rolling in relentlessly, thick, grey, dense roundels of angry, swirling rain-bearing clouds. They held back their rain for much of the day, and Matthias hoped to reach Pevensey Castle before the rains and nightfall, but the ferocious storm broke with vast peals of thunder echoing round the hills surrounding them. Lightning sent daggers of pure white light illuminating the area, giving him a sighting of a heaving grey sea. He caught sight of Pevensey Castle in the distance and knew he must reach it and find shelter. He had ridden over fifteen miles and of necessity must rest. After the thunder, the rain drummed down sending arrows of cold wetness into Matthias' cloak, the wind taking his hat, leaving him no choice but to pull his hood up over his unprotected head. Rain streaked down his face, dripped into his collar, into his eyes making it difficult to see the way ahead. His horse stumbled, and he knew he would have to decrease the pace or risk a tumble.

The final two miles of the journey took too long for his liking. The torrents of water cascaded into the track from the raised mounds on either side of the track soon turning the ground into a river of mud which sucked at his horse's hooves. Several times he was forced to dismount to lead his trembling beast onwards, his boots sinking into the mud and making movement difficult. Lightning continued to flicker eerily round, although the thunder had diminished. Soon he was soaked through to the skin, and Pevensey Castle was a welcome sight.

There was, however, no warm welcome for him. The gates were closed, and the gatekeeper surlily informed him that there was no space for travellers - he would have to go a little further down to Pevensey Haven, where there might be an ale house.

Nearly blinded by the rain, Matthias stumbled down towards the river, where he hoped he would find shelter. He led his horse, anxious lest the rain and rough terrain should cause the animal to stumble. The river was small, but a serviceable harbour had a couple of cogs waiting for the storm to ease, and ale houses, obviously well used by sea farers. With rain dripping off him, Matthias was not a welcome guest anywhere, but he found a shared room in one, and adequate stabling for his horse. Before finding food, Matthias rubbed his mount down himself, talking quietly to it, snickering gently to calm him. A stable boy watched from his seat on an upturned leather bucket.

"Bit of old sack here, mister – you can have that to throw over him."

Matthias accepted it gratefully and turned to go.

"Keep an eye on him for me – we've ridden hard today." He showed the stable boy a coin.

"Thanks mister. I'll be here all night. I sleep here, see."

Matthias' bedfellow was a stout trader waiting to cross the narrow seas on a cog which had been delayed by the storm. He scratched and snored all night, and between the fleas and his snores, Matthias had a poor night so was relieved when the fellow woke early to catch the tide.

His horse was ready for him, saddled by the stable boy who earned another coin. As the horse was led out for Matthias to mount, he noticed another horse snorting and stamping impatiently in the stable.

The boy noticed Matthias looking at him and made a face.

"I have to take him to the castle...He's needed by Sir Melville's guests. One of their horses has gone lame. I don't like going up there – there's always a bit of trouble and you daren't speak in case you get hit."

"I hoped for a bed there yesterday," Matthias said, "but their gate keeper wouldn't let me in."

"There are some bad men there, friends of the castillion – trust me – they knocked me down for speaking to the boy. It's the men who want the horse - one of theirs went lame and they've had to wait a day for this one to be brought down from Willingdon."

"What boy?" Matthias asked, hairs rising on the back of his neck as he said it.

"They've brought a boy with them - they are waiting for the tide and then they will put him on the cog St. Pirran. The storm has dropped so I guess they will bring him down today."

"Would you like to earn some silver?" Matthias asked him.

The stable boy's eyes lit up.

"How could I do that, mister?"

Matthias drew him closer and told him.

Chapter 10

Intervention of an Angel

Luke was woken just after dawn, hustled from the crumbling outhouse in which he had been locked for the night whilst the two men had been welcomed by the castillion of the castle and fed well. They were well acquainted with this man and exchanged news with him as they supped in the privacy of his solar, well away from prying eyes. The storm had delayed them and to further their delay, one of their horses turned lame and prevented them leaving as they wished. A delay of two days would mean the possibility of the cog at Sandwich sailing without the boy. At the castillion's suggestion, they had arranged for Luke to be placed on the St. Pirran, owned by himself – a very satisfactory arrangement.

It was now five weeks since Luke had been abducted; he was thin, dirty, bruised and hungry. Although he had been fed, the fare had mostly consisted of bread, a little cheese and slops of watery soup. The water he had drunk was brackish and gave him a constant griping pain in his stomach. At six years old, he had grown wiser in the last five weeks, less trusting, more wary. He had learned to dodge slaps, keep silent, hold back his tears and remain watchful for any sign of escape, although that hope had faded now. He tried not to think of his mother and Matthias, of his grandsire and grandame and all the friends at home. He knew he would be lucky to see his home again, and thought with longing of the neat schoolroom, the easy life he had led and wondered what now lay ahead of him. The event he tried to block from his mind was the death of Walter on that beach at Shoreham - the great gaping wound in his stomach - the guts -the blood. It made him feel physically sick and he did his best to block it from his memory.

He followed the men obediently out of the castle gates. Pevensey Castle was small and in a poor state of repair. It had been the scene of several sieges, had endured poor management and now was in the hands of this dishonest castillian. The bridge over the moat was broken and to cross was a perilous affair, with one man leading the horse as they descended the small rise to the flat area on which Pevensey Haven was situated. Luke could see the river, winding sluggishly towards the open sea. What had once been a faster flowing river was now steadily silting up; the cogs which were still able to navigate here were smaller and lighter. Soon there would be no sea going vessels able to use this little port.

Although the rain had stopped, the weather was not clear; white tops to the waves far out at sea were visible from the rise from where Luke started. He tried to keep up with the men, afraid of being beaten if he lingered too much behind, but his six-year old legs were weak with fatigue. At the bottom of the hill he passed a young lad idly leaning by a stable door.

"Luke!" he heard, in a throaty whisper.

He turned his head sharply to look at the boy. He didn't know him, but he had definitely heard his name.

"Are you Luke? Nod your head." The boy slid into a walk, following casually behind, talking out of the corner of his mouth.

Luke nodded.

The men were slowing up now.

"Matthias is in the stable with their horse. He is waiting for you but do not speak."

Luke's heart jumped nervously. How had Matthias found him? Was there going to be a fight? He knew he must do exactly as he was told. The men had swords and daggers and one had a businesslike looking arbalest, although it was just hanging on his belt...not primed as far as Luke knew. The men did not expect any trouble.

A roughly dressed man emerged from the stable leading a horse. Luke kept his eyes on the ground.

"Is this the horse for you Sir?" the ostler asked the man who clearly had no mount.

"That's mine, ostler. Could you not have brought it faster? We're in somewhat of an urgent hurry."

"Sorry sir. He was a handful to bring down. Do you want to try him first?"

"Hardly necessary. Do I look as if I would allow a horse to better me?"

"No sir. Sorry sir."

"I'll take him along the harbour and try him just for fun. Watch the boy for me. He's to be handed to the captain of the St. Pirran. Take him along for me...I'll follow to collect payment directly."

Matthias disguised as the ostler couldn't believe his luck. Dressed in sacking and with a filthy hat on his head, he grabbed Luke as soon as they cantered off together down the harbour walk, scattering stall holders and merchandise in their way.

They would have very little time. The stable boy grasped Luke's hand and pulled him away, disappearing fast back through the stable.

"Do as he tells you!" Matthias managed to mutter before Luke disappeared with the stable boy. Matthias darted inside and hastily pulled off the sacking, the hat and donned his own clothes, mounting his own horse and appearing at the stable door as the two men reappeared, laughing together at some ribald jest.

He did not speak to them; just nodded at them as he moved his horse out into the track and began to walk calmly up the path in the direction of Lewes.

The easy part was over and Matthias couldn't believe how smooth it had been. The two men had not expected anything untoward, and had never actually seen him, especially as they had originally been looking for two men – himself and Ezekiel, but now was the risky part.

The two men sauntered down towards the quay, making for the St. Pirran, now preparing to up anchor. Matthias did not dare to look round; to be seen to be watching them would provoke suspicion. He continued on up the incline to re-join the main track back the way he had come.

When he reached the level ground at the top, the way home stretched before him, Lewes, Ovingdean, Shoreham, Arundel, Chichester, Southampton, Salisbury, Shaftesbury - a long, long ride. He suddenly felt unbearably beaten and afraid, but he knew he must walk on with his horse as if he really was one inconspicuous traveller going about his business. He hoped the stable boy would play his part willingly and not double cross him. He was not happy with the feeling that he was walking away from Luke and leaving him to the mercies of a strange family who might see an opportunity to make money out of the situation in which they found themselves.

Luke was weakened from the long journey, poor food and general fear of his situation, so he found the climb up the hill to the place where the boy's mother lived exhausting. He fell a couple of times, grazing his legs on the chalky hillside and breathed with painful gasps, feeling as if his lungs would surely burst. The stable boy, Angel by name, had grasped him by his arm and pulled him rapidly back through the stable, across the yard and then scrambled up the chalky hill, almost a small cliff, to where his mother lived. There, he had thrown Matthias' silver on her table and begged her to put Luke into his own truckle bed. If the house was searched, Luke was a brother with fever - and Angel had disappeared swiftly, knowing he must be back in the stable to behave as an innocent. Angel's mother was a woman of fine fettle – as a fisherman's wife she had to be strong and she had seen many battles with dishonest and cruel seafarers, smugglers and pirates in her time. Her husband had been killed by pirates leaving her with just Angel, and she was quick to respond to his request.

Angel reached the stable moments before the two men roared in, demanding to speak to the ostler, who had not delivered the boy.

"Hold these horses, boy!" one of them shouted at Angel, tossing him the reins as they swept through the ale house demanding the ostler.

It took less than a moment for the two men to realise that there was indeed no ostler, and the boy had disappeared.

Pevensey Haven was a small place and searching for Luke was not difficult. With their bullying and arrogant air, the two, who were known by reputation as part of the feared gang, swept through the poor houses, overturning furniture, breaking sticks of it as they pushed their way into homes, alarming children, scattering fowls, causing mayhem. Angel's home was not exempt. His mother kept her head admirably; she saw them scrambling up the slope, marking their fine clothes with the chalky face of the climb, and taking Luke out of the bed, stripped the meagre bedding from it, making Luke curl up underneath the pile, out of sight.

"The bedding is stained with vomit, sirs," she whined, as they approached the pile, "my son Angel has been sick all night, - he works in the ale house as a stable boy - I have not the strength to touch the foul coverings yet."

Both men grimaced and backed out of the room.

"Ugh – sickness – we need to look elsewhere…"

"Damnable child – he cannot be far."

"Try underneath the moored crafts on the beach, sirs," she warbled, the pretence of being feeble and incompetent working well.

They retreated to the shingle fore shore, and Angel's mother re-instated Luke into the grimy bed.

Grime or no grime, it was a safe place – for now.

The men waited in Pevensey Haven for two days. During that time Matthias did not dare approach the place. He found a hidden shack some way down the track, deserted, tumble-down and cold but near enough for him to return to a vantage point a couple of times during the day to watch the two men search and search again, turning everything inside out. They returned to Pevensey Castle each night angry and frustrated, and on the third day Matthias watched them ride away. Even then he was wary of returning to the little village for fear of trickery by the two, or surveillance by the castillian, who was surely part of their network.

However, return he had to, before dawn on the third day. He had eaten very little over the waiting time and was unshaven, a beard beginning to grow. He felt weak from hunger and thirst, but his main concern was reaching Luke.

Angel was in the stable, his normal sleeping place, and Matthias learned of the huge risk taken by the boy and his mother. The search had been so thorough that Luke had been moved twice, and was now in a cave along the beach, a rocky cave in the chalk cliffs. The final move had been at night and they had had to wait until the tide was out in order to access the cave's entrance. Angel knew about its existence from his father who had smuggled goods once and was relieved to find it empty now. The access to it was only possible at low tide, but the sea did not cover the entrance at high tide, so it was a safe hiding place, although very frightening for a young boy on his own in the dark, hearing the sea grow closer and closer.

Further frustration followed for Matthias as the tide was high at present so he had to wait several hours before he could reach the cave. Whilst waiting, Angel managed to bring some bread and cheese to Matthias, who was not confident enough to show himself to the villagers lest any of them were in the pay of the two men. He lay in a corner of the dingy stable and was aware that he would be smelling of horse dung, mouldy hay and onion, for Angel had brought him onion to accompany his cheese. He worried about his horse, tethered near the shack he had found and hoped it would still be there when he was able to return. He realised he had given little thought to his scholars or even Alice in the last few days, and tried to picture them in his head, distressed that he found himself unable to do so.

Angel went about his normal duties in the humble ale house. Largely used by seafarers coming in to the small harbour, there was little work for a stable lad unless a visitor arrived on horseback for some reason, so he was the boy who did everything from turning the spit to grubbing for vegetables and cleaning the jakes pots. Matthias, half dozing now in the corner, observed that he was a hard worker, complaining never about the many varied tasks he was commanded to do. He was a bright boy, too, knowing that no glance should be thrown in Matthias' direction, not knowing who was left to watch out for the missing boy. The ale-wife was unaware of Matthias' presence, and they both judged it best that it should remain that way.

At low tide Angel decided Matthias should try to reach Luke. He pointed the way carefully but declined to go with him for fear of being missed which would give away Luke's presence. He did manage to provide Matthias with a stolen cold pie and some ale in a leather flagon.

It was fortunate for Matthias that the way over the shingle beach was on the West of the little settlement, so he was unobserved as he rounded the chalky headland and made his way over the wet sand which was revealed at low tide, and hastened round the white rocky foreshore to where he could see the entrance to the cave.

He left the comparatively easy walking on the wet sand as he drew near, needing to climb up the chalky rocks a little way to gain access to the cave.

The sea was a long way out – this was a very low tide on a shallow beach, and as he crossed the beach Matthias realised he had made no plans on how to take Luke out of this cave.

Luke was lying just inside the entrance, obviously preferring the light to the murky darkness further back in the small cave which had the salt smell of the sea, a dankness, a feeling of hopelessness. His eyes were closed and he was not moving.

Matthias knelt down beside him, touched him, felt a fragile warmth. Tears of relief rushed to his eyes and he had to wipe them on the back of his hand. He touched him again, more firmly and said his name gently. The child stirred and mumbled something. He was thin, dressed in a filthy brown tunic, tattered hose and had bare feet which were protruding through the hose, his feet having been cut by scrambling over rocks, shoeless. There was a livid bruise visible on one shoulder, and Matthias noticed his fingernails were torn, ragged and dirty. His breathing was irregular and shuddering.

He put his arms round the frail body and lifted him up, taking off his own cloak and wrapping it round Luke, holding him close, his own unshaven face close to the child's smooth one, and found himself whispering endearments to him.

He sat like that for some time, heedless of the tide, rocking the child tenderly, willing him to speak.

As warmth crept back into him, Luke stirred in Matthias' arms.

"I'm sorry," he croaked hoarsely.

Chapter 11

The Nightmare Continues

The household at Barton Holding was now seriously concerned for the safety of Matthias with the possibility of Luke being found receding into the distance.

Alice grew pale as the days passed and Martin tried his best to keep her spirits up, but she grew snappy with him, then hated herself for being so. She knew he was trying to do the best for her, but she found it hard to hold her head up and continue with Matthias' work. Martin was becoming anxious to make his move but realised that if Matthias did not return, this might alter his situation.

Sir Tobias and Lady Bridget began to call more frequently, anxious of what the future might hold and to support their daughter as well as they could. Sir Tobias had work which could not be neglected and tried to put his heart into his work. Felonies were meagre compared to the tragedy which appeared to have engulfed his own family and the news of Luke's disappearance was now a topic of gossip in the village, and even in Sherborne where Sir Tobias was known.

Alice detested this and instructed Martin and Lydia to be open in their conversations in order that the villagers would know the true sequence of events rather than embroidered gossip.

Ezekiel and Martha came daily to uphold the feeling of hope, but as the weeks progressed, Ezekiel admitted to Martin and Davy that it was beginning to look extremely black.

Alice took to spending time before the scholars' arrival on her knees in the little church, praying fervently for her husband, her young son and confessing her own inadequacy. She tried to leave her crushing sadness behind her as she approached the house, knowing Davy and Elizabeth would be watching over her. It gave her some relief to realise that she put her husband and her son on the same level - no longer was she doubting her ability to be Matthias' wife. In an odd way, this gave her the strength to continue to keep faith that they would return.

The miserable Summer had turned to Autumn, the damp weather continued, and Elizabeth remarked one day that food amongst the population was going to be scarce this Winter. This, the second wet Summer in succession, was causing discontent and poverty throughout the land.

Sir Tobias was alarmed at the rumours of unrest further East in the country, fuelled by famine and disease, with the King still not willing to impose his stamp of authority on the quarrelsome lords. England was no longer a contented prosperous island it would seem. Power struggles between Cardinal Beaufort and Lord Suffolk continued whilst the King was growing used to allowing others to make decisions on his behalf. Suffolk had become a powerful influence in the land, whilst the young king showed more interest in education, the arts and architecture. It was abundantly clear that he would never follow his father's leadership on the battlefield.

Sherborne was largely unaffected by this, the rebuilding of the fire-affected parts of the Abbey progressing, although more slowly than the Abbot would have wished. The almshouse was going up faster than the Abbey repairs, and this irked Abbot Bradford no end.

Merrik was still in Sherborne. He found the peace of the Abbey restorative; he loved to sit and watch Edric carving his wood, caressing it from time to time with his skilful fingers.

He had returned once to Bradford by Avon when the player's carts returned there, but his visit was a sad one. In his absence, his sister had been found guilty of assisting the now vanished Walter the Woodman in his killing spree, and she was hanged. Sir Tobias was unable to help him for this was out of his domain and he had no jurisdiction in that area. Merrik had returned a sadder man, quieter, subdued, looking for a purpose, and frequented the Abbey daily, praying always for the return of Walter so that he could face justice.

It seemed impossible to Sir Tobias that life could continue as if nothing untoward had happened when his small world had collapsed so completely, grief and uncertainty touching their everyday lives. His beloved grandson appeared to be beyond help, his daughter's second husband was unaccounted for and as the days now stretched into weeks the bleakness of her position caused him pain.

It was amazing to Alice that she managed to keep the school operating. There were eight scholars excluding Luke, and Ennis still attended in the afternoons. She was fortunate in the families they served; so far, and it had now been four weeks since Ezekiel had returned, they had remained totally supportive, and the boys had continued to prosper.

Ezekiel was burdened by the thought that he should not have left Matthias and tried to manage his own work without speaking aloud his feeling of dread for the fate of his friend and the child. He had spoken only to Sir Tobias of the ruthlessness of the smugglers, the cruelty, the high stakes for which they played, and Sir Tobias knew in his heart that he must inform the King of such gangs who were cheating him out of taxes and terrorising the South coast, but he could not do so whilst there was a chance of Luke's return. If there was the slightest hope that Matthias had managed to find him, that must not be jeopardised.

Towards the end of September he decided that it was time to seek audience at court to inform the King's clerks of what he knew, and with a heavy heart, he and William began to prepare for their journey.

Matthias did not return to Pevensey Haven, deeming it too dangerous. Angel had told him of a cliff path which would lead him very close to the place where he had left his horse.

However, his first concern was the condition of Luke. He couldn't say, afterwards, how long he had sat cradling Luke, rocking him like a young baby, comforting him with soft words and gentle touches. He certainly missed the next tide for he heard the sound of the waves coming closer, felt the chill of the evening sea breeze and smelt the salty tang of the sea.

He quickly became chilled himself, having wrapped Luke in his cloak, so he wedged himself, still cradling the child, against a boulder which afforded him some protection from the breeze, and hugged Luke to him, taking a little warmth from the child's body, and so they stayed until morning.

Daylight brought rain, slashing down in vicious streaks, driving into the mouth of the cave forcing Matthias to move back to the darker more protective part. Luke woke and struggled to sit up, stiff from the sheer effort of so many days walking, trudging, hurrying, saddle-sore from being thrown roughly over the saddle of one or other of the men. The effort Matthias had made to warm him and comfort him had reduced his shivering although he was still weak, his voice cracked and sore.

Matthias broke a small piece of the pie Angel had given him and raised the ale flagon to Luke's parched lips. He tried to swallow some ale, but it trickled out of his mouth, the action of swallowing causing him discomfort. Matthias moistened his swollen lips with a little of the ale and tried again. This time Luke managed a small amount of the liquid. Matthias took a mouthful himself and ate a little of the pie, thankful for the rough pastry and greasy filling, despite it being hardly suitable to give to Luke.

A sound outside gave him cause for alarm...someone was approaching, the scrambling sound of feet negotiating the rocky cliff face made slippery by the rain. His relief when the wet face of Angel appeared in the cave entrance was tangible.

Angel was wet through, rain streaming off him, panting from his exertions towards the cave. He had brought oatmeal, moistened with a little milk - once hot but cold now, infinitely better for Luke.

He told Matthias that although the two men had ridden off and had not returned, there was still a danger from the dishonest castillion, who had sheltered the men, probably part of the chain. Matthias was too tired to think properly and wondered what the next move should be.

Angel suggested moving up the cliff path to the place where the horse had been tethered, and Matthias was inclined to agree. A horse left tethered untended for too long was a temptation to anyone who happened upon it.

Angel did not dare stay long for fear of being missed and loped back down towards the wide beach through the driving rain, leaving Matthias with the little pot of oatmeal.

The rain had stopped, although the sky was an unfriendly grey, threatening more downpours as Matthias crouched at the mouth of the cave looking out towards an equally unfriendly sea. What should he do? Luke was certainly in no state to walk but they needed to be away from here and reclaim his mount before some other stranger found it and took it.

The tide was on the turn; soon it would be impossible to return to Pevensey Haven by foot until the next tide. Matthias looked upwards at the chalk cliff. At this point it was not very high and offered many easy looking foot holds. He debated with himself. Luke was not heavy; if he was able to hold on to Matthias it should be possible to climb the cliff just above the cave, which he thought probably joined the path near to where he had left his horse.

Feeding Luke the oatmeal carefully with his horn spoon, Matthias spoke softly and slowly to the child.

"Luke, you've been very brave. We have to try and go home, but I need you to do exactly as I say. I am going to carry you on my back so that we can climb the cliff together. It will be wet so some of the rocks will be slippery. You have to hold on tight. If you slip away from me, grab the vegetation and hold on. I will come back for you."

The child looked at Matthias with glazed eyes, hardly focussing on Matthias at all, so he was not at all sure that Luke had understood.

"Luke, we need to go on an adventure to reach home, like Alexander the Great."

Luke's eyes came into focus; the mention of a classroom story, although hardly relevant, had broken into his nightmare. He nodded.

Matthias finished feeding him, wrapped his cloak firmly round the child's body and crouched down to allow Luke to slip his arms round Matthias' shoulders. Standing up with the boy on his back didn't feel very secure to Matthias, but he was aware of the tiny hands gripping together round his neck, nearly choking him.

"Not quite so tight, Luke - I need to breathe."

On a fine day, this climb would have been little more than a scramble up a cliff which was not particularly high, - the height began further round the coast. This section was much lower, leading down towards the harbour. On a wet day with an unsteady, precarious burden on his back, it seemed endless to Matthias, slipping once or twice and dislodging chalk boulders as he clutched at possible hand holds. Luke's hands gripped even more tightly as Matthias struggled to find suitable holds. Once they both slid back a few feet, stones and wet vegetation falling below them. Matthias' hands were raw, for he had lost his gauntlets long ago on the journey. As they neared the top it began to rain again, a steady drizzle more saturating than the heavier rain of the morning. Hauling himself and the child up those last few yards seemed the hardest part, and for a few moments Matthias lay on the wet path, breathing heavily, his lungs fit to burst. Luke allowed himself to roll off Matthias' back and crouched over Matthias' exhausted form lying on the path.

"Please don't die, Matthias," he whimpered. Matthias pulled himself upright, hugging Luke to him, reassuring him.

"My arms and legs are weak from climbing...that's all... let's go and find Bucephalas. Can you walk a little?"

The mention of Alexander's horse brought a weak smile to Luke's pinched face. He staggered to his feet and pushed his hand into Matthias' cold one.

"I can do whatever you want me to," he said through his swollen sore lips.

Together they braved the track, seeking Bucephalas.

Sir Tobias and his squire William were readying themselves for a journey. Sir Tobias was much more concerned now for his son-in-law and grandson than he would allow anyone to see. He guessed Matthias would be short of coin by now, if indeed he was still alive, and his horse would surely be spent - It was time the King's clerks learned of this smuggling and sent royal clerks to investigate.

Since becoming a Justice of the Peace Sir Tobias had learned more regarding the workings of the king's court. He had always understood the complicated system of spying for the royal court, with highly placed courtiers employing spies and messengers in all parts of the realm as well as abroad. He had himself been in a position of trust when in France fighting under King Henry Vth and was disappointed in the lack of responsibility shown now by this House of Lancaster, sparring frequently among those who supported the Duke of York. With the young king unwilling to exert his kingship it was left to courtiers such as the Duke of Suffolk, William de la Pole, to attempt to keep a steady hand on government.

The court was currently at Windsor, and with six days riding behind them, Sir Tobias found himself waiting in an ante room for an audience with William de la Pole, Duke of Suffolk.

As a knight, Sir Tobias did have dignity and station, although lowly enough for the Duke to keep him waiting for a whole day, and to think to give him but little of his time.

However, William de la Pole's grandfather had been a wealthy and influential wool merchant in Hull, and the smuggling of wool had been instrumental in the downfall of the English Wool Company a century ago.

As Sir Tobias gave a succinct account of as much of the story as he could ascertain with any certainty, de la Pole's face darkened, his frown changed his visage from a politely interested look to a narrowing of eyes, a squaring of shoulders, a more piercing perception of the situation than Sir Tobias had hoped.

They were in a sumptuously decorated ante room, gold angels painted on the ceiling, beeswax candles lighting the room and causing the gold of the angels with their fat cheeks and flowing hair to reflect glimmers of light on the flagged floor. No furnishings in this room, but Suffolk ushered Sir Tobias into a further room leading off the anteroom in which there was a spacious desk with two royal clerks industriously poring over documents.

Sir Tobias, black hose pushed into high heeled riding boots, a black leather jerkin reaching his thighs, belted with a fine leather belt, sword buckled, felt underdressed beside Suffolk, richly attired in a white linen undershirt, dark red houppelande embroidered round the hem and cuffs, soft court shoes gleaming with jewels and his beringed hands speaking of riches and prosperity. His hair was oiled and perfumed, a chain denoting his office hung round his neck, and at his entry the two clerks sat up deferentially, their eyes wary, waiting for whatever was to come.

"Map!" he snapped.

One of the clerks reached for a scroll taken from a locked chest behind the desk.

The parchment scroll was large, and as the two clerks unrolled it and placed it over the whole desk, Sir Tobias gazed in wonderment at the unfolding mysteries of the whole of England. Tiny settlements were inked in, the cursive, careful script of the makers in black, tracks in red, rivers and other areas of water in green. Gold pigment decorated the edges, castles highlighted with gold. Truly this map was the work of highly trained scribes who must have worked painstakingly for hours, information being fed in by trained observers who had ridden the trackways, listed settlements, investigated castles, monasteries, asked the name of rivers, lakes, villages. The work of years, the pride of its owners, England, Scotland and Wales were all represented, even going as far as Calais, still owned by the English crown.

"Fifty years old, Sir Tobias," the duke informed him, a touch of pride in his voice.

He bent over the parchment, indicating with a well-manicured hand the city of Hull.

"My grandfather was a successful wool merchant here when I was a boy. The wool smugglers were rife then, and it appears they are still rife today, cheating the crown out of taxes."

He moved round the desk, the better to view the South coast. The cursive script of the text was clear to read; Sir Tobias picked out Salisbury, with the cathedral showing the height of its spire, and his eyes followed the red marks depicting tracks, taking in Chichester, Arundel Shoreham, Lewes, and so on, right round to Canterbury and Sandwich.

"Your lady wife has connections with Canterbury, I believe," Sir Tobias commented, daring the familiar touch.

Suffolk fixed a gimlet glance in his direction, but a glimmer of a smile crossed his lips.

"In a manner of speaking, I suppose she does," was his wry response.

Sir Tobias was aware that William de la Pole was married to Alice Chaucer, the granddaughter of the poet, who had made Canterbury well known amongst educated men for more than just its place as the prime place of worship in the whole of England, and a place of pilgrimage. His witty and sometimes irreverent tales of the pilgrimage were loved by some and hated by others.

"This business needs resolving. The King will not like this tale of ruthless cruelty on his coast, let alone the loss of taxes. I doubt your grandson to be still living, but I will send a party of King's men to flush out the coven of smugglers. We thank you for your information."

Sir Tobias flinched at the cold soulless assumption that Luke was already lost to them. He allowed himself to study the map more closely, noticing with dread how far Luke may have been taken.

"Will there be any possibility of assistance in returning the boy to Sherborne should the king's men find him?"

"What kind of assistance is in your mind?"

"He is hardly seven Summers old. If Master Barton has failed to find him, he will be alone, bewildered, shocked, injured…"

William de la Pole cut him short with a wave of his impatient hand.

"I will instruct them to do whatever they see fit to do."

A swirl of his rich red robe and he was gone. The two clerks relaxed.

"Look more closely at this map, Sir Tobias," they offered.

Sir Tobias did so, noting that he could reach Lewes or Shoreham fairly directly from Windsor. He looked searchingly at the scroll, striving to remember all the intricate details on it.

The clerks became nervous, afraid of Sir William returning, and Sir Tobias took his leave, searching for his squire and his horse, knowing where he was bound for now.

Chapter 12

Brother Jerome's Advice

Matthias and Luke rested in the ramshackle building where thankfully the horse was still tethered. Luke, still weak and shocked, insisted that the horse was now called Bucephalus. Matthias smiled wanly, too exhausted and chilled to argue, but thankful that Luke had spoken, for he had said very little since Matthias had found him.

The September nights were damp but not particularly cold mercifully, leaving Matthias able to wrap the child in his cloak which was now drying, and find a corner of the building sheltered from any night winds which might blow. Looking down on Luke's white face, purple shadows under his half-closed eyes, lips still swollen and dry from lack of water, Matthias felt for the first time the weight of responsibility for another human being.

With no further words, Luke slipped into an uneasy sleep. Matthias was too worried to sleep. He felt cold, although the night was not especially chilly, but he had been soaked by rain, drenched in his own sweat which had dried uncomfortably on his body, and was now without his cloak, so just in his jerkin shirt and hose. His boots were wet and unpleasant to wear but he was afraid to take them off in case he couldn't get them on again. Luke had bare feet he noted, feet which looked cut and bruised.

He half dozed for a little, waking as Luke cried out in fear. He cradled the boy in his arms, saying his name over and over until he fell into further sleep.

Matthias was aware of their perilous position. He had used the very last of his silver to persuade Angel and his mother to help them, and although he instinctively felt they were trustworthy, he could not be sure that they would not seek him to hope for more silver for their silence.

He was also mindful of the distance they had travelled. With no coin and no friends on this part of the coast, how was he going to proceed home? He had been away for nearly two months - Ezekiel would have been home for five weeks - what would be going through Alice's mind? His mount, too, had suffered from lack of good care - he had no fodder, only the meagre grazing found wherever they had halted.

Luke cried out many times during this long night. Matthias gave up any attempt to sleep, holding Luke close in his arms, murmuring words of comfort to him until dawn broke.

He moved a short distance away from the shack as morning dawned to relieve himself, encouraging Luke to do the same. He had to help the child stand, for his limbs were stiff and painful. He became aware that Luke's clothes were stained with vomit and urine, there were flea bites all over his body and his head was itching. Ruefully he acknowledged to himself that he too would soon itch and have flea bites having cradled Luke so closely.

Suddenly he was alarmed to hear the steady approach of another human being. He tentatively drew his knife from its sheath, crouching ready to attack if necessary, protecting Luke with his body.

A deep quiet steady voice spoke from outside the ruined place.

"Pax et Bonum,"

"Pax et Bonum" Matthias replied, shuddering with relief, as a black garbed friar appeared, leaning on a stout staff, his thin face etched with the pain of climbing the path from Pevensey Haven, his piercing blue eyes under sparse black eyebrows taking in the two of them.

"My son, I believe you are in need of help," he said, entering their shelter.

He was tall, thin, his strong veined hands resting on the staff he used to help him with the climb. An aura of calm surrounded this Dominican friar. He caught sight of Luke, crouched trembling behind Matthias and sketched a blessing over him.

"There is no need to fear, my child. Angel asked me to help you."

Matthias stood up, re-sheathing his knife.

"I have no more silver to give," he told the friar, who held up one bony hand in protest.

"No payment is necessary. You need shelter before you take your next journey. The child has been much misused, and you yourself need sustenance. Wilmington Priory will help you. It is some seven miles from here. A small priory, you will find rest there, - tell them Brother Jerome sent you."

The friar gave instructions in his clear, dignified manner, making sure Matthias understood the route he should take and what he should say on arrival, and then left as abruptly as he had arrived.

Matthias gathered up Luke and the few items he had used from his pack, mounted Bucephalus with Luke in front of him, and the weary party left Pevensey Haven behind them.

Sir Tobias and his squire William left Windsor in the company of two king's men, both royal clerks, well- armed and with a small company of archers. Their journey was an easier ride than they realised. Flying the royal banner meant other travellers on the road had to make way for them, and the royal clerks did not stand on ceremony. They comman-deered rooms for the night easily, high up on the Hogs Back, already half-way to the coast.

The captain of archers was a Welshman, garrulous, with a merry grin and an eye for the ladies. After a dish of mutton heavily laced with spices, he disappeared with a wink at his fellow archers, leaving Sir Tobias and William with his cohort, blackjacks of ale all round. The royal clerks had taken themselves to their room, preferring their own company.

Sir Tobias was wary of spilling too much information. He and William were both old hands on military expeditions and knew that too much talking in too public a place could lead to disaster. However, the archers knew enough about their destination to glean snippets from Sir Tobias, who made it clear to the archers that he and William were not really part of their number, travelling with them specifically for protection in order to attempt to find the boy.

The archers told him that they were bound first for Lewes and would then make their way along the coast towards Sandwich, on the Kent coast.

Sir Tobias felt he and William would rather start at Shoreham, where Ezekiel had last seen Matthias.

The following day they parted company with the royal clerks and their party of archers and followed the course of the River Adur down to Shoreham.

Sir Tobias was dismayed to find they could uncover no useful information in Shoreham. He sought out the port reeve, but he denied any evidence of smuggling or of death on the shore. The shifty look in his eyes as he spoke with the Coroner told a different story, but Sir Tobias was anxious to push on with their journey – leave the close questioning to the royal clerks, he decided. Local fishermen told the same story, and by the third day, Sir Tobias and William rode on to Lewes, hoping they might catch up with the party they had left. In this they were of course disappointed, as Sir Tobias had lingered too long in Shoreham, allowing the royal clerks to move ahead of them.

Lewes was a little more rewarding. They sought shelter at the Cluniac priory of Lewes, and were much encouraged by the sympathetic ear of the Prior, who admitted that he had heard of such gangs who worked the coastal routes with wool and other items of contraband, - all to the detriment of the King.

Since Cluny was in France, the priory was known as an alien house, but Sir Tobias and his squire experienced nothing but kindly hospitality and well- meaning advice on how they should proceed. The prior had forgotten that Matthias had sought shelter with them for one night so no mention was made of this to Sir Tobias, who asked for information about two travellers, mistakenly believing that Ezekiel was still with Matthias at this point.

The priory had suffered debt and hardship in the preceding years, due no doubt to the revolt led by the men of Kent and Wat Tyler, still in the memory of some older people. The Coroner learned of the cruelty, poverty, desperation and despair of the folk of Kent and Sussex during that time, and the disregard some of them felt for the king, even now.

Resentment was bubbling in the shires yet again.

In the hope that Matthias might have sought shelter in other monastic houses, they left the next morning, bound for Michelham, an Augustinian priory, where the prior, one Thomas Wynchelse, welcomed them somewhat austerely, his priory being small and like so many others in this area, debt ridden. He listened in silence to their story, but to their disappointment he could offer no crumb of hope. Matthias clearly had not passed through this priory, or it seemed, any other monastic place of shelter.

They left messages with the gate keeper in case there was a chance that Matthias sought shelter there, but continued towards Battle Abbey, some twenty miles further on.

Sir Tobias had begun to wonder whether he had chosen the right course to follow. It appeared to him sensible that Matthias might have used monastic houses to help him on his way, as their duty was to give shelter to travellers in need, but so far there was no evidence to support his idea; they picked up no trace of him, and whilst most folk to whom they spoke acknowledged the existence of smuggling gangs working the coastal towns, no one was prepared to engage in talk about their whereabouts or activities.

They were now four days out of London and beginning to feel despondent. The rain began again, a chill wind blew off the sea, and Sir Tobias' great mare fell lame. Suddenly, the Coroner felt his age creep upon him insidiously; William glanced sideways at him and saw his despair and indecision. He dismounted and took the reins of the mare.

"We must seek shelter and re-plan, Sir Tobias. Remember France? Find a solution, you told me. Don't bring me problems, - bring me solutions. So, let us find a solution!"

Matthias and Luke found rest and care at the tiny priory of Wilmington. For Matthias the journey had been little short of a nightmare. Luke was clearly much affected by his experiences, and it was difficult to break through his ramblings and mutterings which were full of detail concerning Walter's injuries. The graphic descriptions which Luke gave in a broken, hoarse whisper were horrific, - things which few six year-old boys should witness, although Matthias was aware that life for many people was harsh and some children grew to expect such sights as part of their lives. Luke had lived a protected and loved life, soft living surrounding him in the gentle village of Stour Caundle.

Twice on the journey he vomited the oats Matthias had carefully spooned into him, and the door keeper monk was certainly much credited for his speed when admitting them to the priory, although wrinkling his nose as Matthias carried Luke into a small whitewashed cell with a pristine bed with clean coverings. A brother soon appeared bearing a pitcher of warm water and cloths with which to wash the child and as Matthias stripped Luke of his befouled garments, the Prior himself appeared. Matthias mentioned Brother Jerome, and the Prior's craggy face softened.

"Brother Jerome is our eyes in this part of the world," he told Matthias, watching as he bathed Luke's poor body with warm water, as gently as he could.

"There has been much unrest in the East of the shire, and into Kent. We are an alien house, unconnected with the mother church in England, so we need to understand the mood of the populace. Brother Jerome is a Dominican friar – not one of our order, but he feeds us such news as he thinks important. We have learned of these gangs, but they have not affected us. They have no interest in our prayers and offices."

Matthias threw Luke's garments into a corner of the room.

"I will wash his clothes myself if you could provide me with water and a suitable vessel."

"That will not be necessary. I will send for our washer-woman to deal with them. Meanwhile, wrap the child in this tunic. He is much disturbed in his humours. We have an apothecary brother. Let me send him to you."

Matthias was more than grateful for the administrations of the good brother who examined Luke with tenderness, prepared a salve for his bruises, attended to his cut feet and left a bowl of fragrant herbs lit by a candle beneath. The aroma was pleasant, soporific and Matthias dozed as he sat exhausted on the floor by the bed, intending to watch Luke, but soon falling asleep himself.

When the Brother returned with the washerwoman to collect Luke's garments, he was pleased to observe the two sleeping forms, calmed by the burning herbs which would soothe the mind.

Alice woke with a feeling of dread despair. The wet Summer had turned into a wet Autumn; she lay in the great fourposter bed she and Matthias had shared, wept for her short life as the wife of Matthias, who had been away too long now for any good to come of this. Her heart bled for the loss of her beautiful son, but equally for the loss of her husband, who had tried so hard to make the family a complete unit. She was thankful that Titus had confessed to his taunting, for it meant that Titus' father was championing Alice's efforts at keeping the scholars on their path to learning. Without him, Alice felt she would have lost one or two scholars by now, although in truth, there was little else for them at present.

As the days passed, she tried desperately to keep her pain to herself. It would do no good to worry her lady mother, fretting herself now Sir Tobias and William had ridden away. Martin did not deserve to have her fears foisted on his shoulders spoiling his hopes of a new life with Lydia, and Davy and Elizabeth were as anxious as she was herself, each day bringing greater uncertainty.

She scrubbed her eyes dry on the bolster and sat up. Daylight filtered into the room as she swung her legs onto the floor. Suddenly a feeling of strength and determination surged through her veins. Yes – that was an answer! She would have to make decisions and act on them. What a brave, bold idea!

The bold idea was to plan Martin's marriage feast to free the barn and allow her to plan an expansion. Secretly she wondered whether she was being too devious – she couldn't bring herself to admit that it was not for Martin's happiness, but for her ability to expand, and maybe - yes - maybe - admit one or two girls.

She would speak to Martin today she decided as she slipped her night shift over her head and reached for her under-garments.

Later, when the scholars were enjoying their bread and cheese, she broached the idea to Martin.

"Lady Alice -" he exclaimed, shocked, "I couldn't!"

"Why?" She kept her gaze steadily on Martin, fixing him with her fierce expression.

"I have to face facts, Martin. As the days go by it seems more than likely that Matthias has met with disaster," even with her resolve high she could not bring herself to use the word death, "and he would not want you to give up the chance of happiness with Lydia. I know it would be hard, but to begin with I would need you to come every day to help me with the scholars, but Davy would help you mount the nag.

You have used it before with little difficulty. I will ask my lady mother for the loan of another small horse from their stables."

Martin could sense her excitement and promised to talk the idea over with Lydia. Meanwhile, Alice moved on to Davy and Elizabeth with her idea and also to Ezekiel when he rode over to collect his boys.

At first it was uphill work, but after a few days, the plan took shape and Alice took Martin and Lydia to see the priest. The date was set for October 28th, celebrating the feast day of St. Simon and St, Jude.

Alice thought how very appropriate this was, St. Jude being the patron saint of hope and impossible causes.

Chapter 13

A Healing for Matthias

September moved into October; the evenings grew darker. Matthias was becoming more and more concerned about their prolonged absence and his inability to make plans for a return to Dorset.

Luke healed, but slowly; he was able to eat now without vomiting his food; his feet had healed somewhat – Matthias had fashioned a simple covering for his feet which did at least give some warmth, although they were not strong enough to be able to walk far without the fabric quickly becoming worn. What was slower to heal was his mind. Matthias had a cot set up close to Luke's and was up several times each night holding him close, calming his cries.

He, Matthias, had healed himself, - sleep and food had seen to that. He had relished the balm of warm water, a little piece of soap and the ability to have his clothes cleaned. The monks had taken the horse into their stables and now, a week after their arrival, the horse too was rested and better fed.

Matthias sat in their chapel, listening to the daily services and finding a sort of peace of mind for which he was grateful yet despite this, thoughts teemed through his head. Was Luke ready to move yet? He hardly thought so, but how could they remain here, far from their home and leaving Alice in doubt and pain. Without money how would they manage – Matthias had very little remaining in his purse now. By land, the journey was some twelve to fourteen days riding, and that didn't take into account Luke's weak state. Might it be better to try for a sea voyage? If they could reach Lewes, they might find a ship travelling with goods to Poole, and then the journey was just a day, but no captain would take two passengers and his horse without payment.

Matthias left the serenity of the chapel and returned to the little room he and Luke occupied. Luke had dressed himself in his newly laundered clothes, rather shabbier than when he had left home, but still his own clothes. Matthias was pleased to see the effort Luke had made. It was the first time he had left the bed without Matthias urging him to do so.

"Shall we go and feed Bucephalus?" Matthias suggested. Luke nodded. He kept his head down, eyes never meeting those of Matthias.

They went slowly to the stable block, Matthias ever mindful of the strips of cloth binding Luke's feet.

Bucephalus whinnied and snickered to them softly, restless today. Matthias knew he needed some exercise, but he was unwilling to leave Luke on his own. Luke nuzzled the horse's nose, rubbing his head against the softness.

"I lost my pony, Matthias," he said very quietly. Matthias held his breath. It was one of the first things Luke had said about his ordeal. He was careful to answer in the right way.

"When we reach home, we can see if we can find him, Luke." He didn't want to suggest simply buying him another – it didn't seem the right thing to do.

"I lost Ezekiel's dagger too."

"Ezekiel's dagger?"

"Ezekiel must have been on the beach with those men – his dagger was there. Was he killed too?"

"Ezekiel went back to Dorset to wait for us there – his dagger was stolen from the house."

"There was a lot of blood, Matthias. Where was Ezekiel?"

Matthias sat down on a pile of straw and pulled Luke down with him, and in the darkness of the stable at Wilmington Priory, the familiar smell of horse, hay and wet rain assailing their senses, Luke's confusion and fears that his friend's father had been part of the gang, had been killed, was not to be trusted, that somehow Matthias was not what he seemed, tumbled from him in broken sentences. Half sobbing, he gasped and shuddered at the terrible memories of the trudging walk behind the pack ponies, having to bear the agony of cut feet, the beatings, the snarls of men he did not know when Walter was not near him, the disgust he felt when having to urinate and defaecate in the open country side, the filth of his own body when he was unable to prevent himself from vomiting with fear, the loss of his pony, the terrifying ride from Barton Holding, the nights of sleeping in uncomfortable places, his inability to escape when the Woodman bought a local girl's body and enjoyed her while lying next to Luke and finally the worst he could ever imagine, the body of the Woodman, almost gutted by a knife, blood and entrails beginning to spill out as he watched in horror, looking at Ezekiel's knife lying near the man.

Eventually Luke's whispered, broken, half incoherent account came to an end and Matthias tightened his arms round the trembling child. He had not spoken of his ordeal to anyone, and the relief of pouring it out to some-one was cathartic.

Matthias stayed where he was, Luke leaning against him, spent with the agony of re-living it all.

"Luke, I came to find you, with Ezekiel. We have been searching for over two months now. I was so lucky to find you. What would we do without you?"

It was all Matthias needed to say. He felt Luke's tears against his face as Luke pushed his face up close to Matthias and kissed his cheek.

William was quick to sense the desperation in Sir Tobias and sought to find a solution before the age of the Coroner began to tell against their journey. Leading the mare, the two men made their way towards a fork in the track. A field worker was attempting to harvest root vegetables in the sodden soil. William accosted him with enquiries, and re-joined the Coroner, now wiping the sweat from his face, for walking on this muddy track was certainly no great pleasure.

"There is a small monk's cell down this track – Otham Priory. We will see what help they can offer us."

Otham turned out to be very small, quite bare, two or three monks only in residence, but nevertheless it was the solution William had been seeking. A bed, rest for the animals and news of exactly where they were.

The Coroner considered whether they should continue or return home, having no news of import, for he was painfully aware of his own duties in Dorset, and had not realised how long any pursuit would take. William noted his musing with a wry smile, - Sir Tobias was becoming forgetful of the long campaign journeys!

"We should not have chased down here, but I cannot bear the feeling that my grandson is being held somewhere and I am unable to help him," he grumbled, pushing meat vegetables and gravy around in his trencher without any true appetite for the food.

Brother Clement, the senior brother in this priory, spoke to them before the Grand Silence began.

"There is a large stable at a neighbouring priory, with possibly better healing for your mount, but you will have to walk the distance. It is at Wilmington, some six miles from here. Like ours, it is small, although not as small as this. If you take the lame mare, leaving early tomorrow, you may be able to heal her sufficiently to move on."

William offered to take the mare, being more able to walk the distance than Sir Tobias, and without further discussion, the decision was made, - William would take the lame mare to Wilmington on the morrow, and then they would sadly make for home.

Alice had started her preparations for Martin and Lydia's nuptials. Planning a way forward eased her troubled soul and

Father Stephen, their parish priest, was glad to see a more peaceful acceptance within her as she knelt at the early morning mass. He had seen Lydia's first husband buried, had known Matthias' mother and father and sisters and was praying daily for the return of the missing parties, but as the days went on it did seem as if October 28th was truly the right day to hold Martin and Lydia's nuptials, the festival of impossible causes.

Alice asked Ezekiel to ride into Sherborne for her and seek out the man Merrik, about whom her father had spoken. He had been involved with a troupe of players and remembering Matthias' comment about dancing not being tactful towards Martin, she had a whim to invite the travelling players to celebrate the day, if she could locate them.

Ezekiel requested Martin to accompany him, and Alice was happy to move all the scholars in together for one day, so with Martin riding the nag and Ezekiel on his own mount, they rode into Sherborne to seek Merrik.

Ezekiel had an idea for Martin which he wanted to explore; he had seen some of Martin's carving work, very detailed despite his partial sight. He had heard Sir Tobias talk about the carving of the misericords in the Abbey, and he had a mind to take Martin into the Abbey to watch the carver for a while.

They found Merrik without much difficulty and Ezekiel explained what Alice had in mind. Merrik was a big, mournful man, the more so since his sister's execution and the failure to find Walter the Woodman. He felt an affinity with this family, for it was the loss of the grandson which bothered him greatly; it added to Walter's mortal sins – for which truly Merrik wished him to hang and rot in hell for ever. Merrik knew where to find the players and their cart and promised to do so, leaving Ezekiel and Martin free to call in to the Abbey.

Martin hadn't been down to Sherborne since the day of the fire, and he was interested to see the scaffolding, but it appeared that the almshouse was forging ahead with more goodwill than the Abbey repairs.

Ezekiel found an urchin to mind their horses. The wet Summer had delayed the re-building, and the Winter thatch was being readied to protect the interior during the Winter months. There was still work going on inside the cavernous Abbey; Martin steadied himself carefully on his crutches and squinted up to the roof with his good eye. The symmetry, the beauty was unbelievable. It caught in his throat in its perfection. Looking up in such a way disturbed his balance, and he would have stumbled had Ezekiel not steadied him. He shook his head to clear his limited vision, and to his amazement he found he could see a little more with his blind side.

He gasped.

"What is it?" Ezekiel asked him in hushed tones.

"My eye! Looking up in that way with my neck so stretched has released a little vision on my blind side. It's like a miracle!"

Ezekiel turned him to face him. He held out three fingers and with his other hand covered Martin's good eye.

"How may fingers can you see?" he demanded.

"Three."

Ezekiel kept his hand over Martin's good eye and pointed towards the workmen on the scaffolding.

"How many men on the first level?"

Martin had to screw his eye up, but he could make out three figures working on the platform, not very distinctly, but they were more than just blobs.

"Three - three Ezekiel – what has happened? Will it stay?"

"You must have unleashed a partial nerve in the eye. I cannot say whether it will stay, but it is certainly like a miracle – especially in a place such as this. Enjoy it, Martin. You deserve it."

Martin would have dearly liked to fall to his knees in thanks for a miracle, but that was impossible for him, so with eyes brimming with delighted tears, they moved in awe down the nave to where Edric was working.

Martin watched in excited wonder as Edric worked, oblivious to the watching men as he plied his chisel, delicately picking out a fruit. Martin moved closer to see better and Edric finished the stroke of his tool and turned to glare at them.

"Forgive me," Martin stammered, "I am a wood carver myself, but not of your skill. I have been told of this work; I wanted to see it for myself."

A rare smile lit Edric's face. It transformed him, gave him a light within himself. He found himself inviting Martin to step closer to inspect the finished misericord and touch the one on which he was working. The two men exchanged words on preferred tools, woods, and as Edric realised the extent of Martin's injuries, he was moved to place a tool in his hands with which to fashion a mark on his work. His apprentice watched with bated breath. Edric was a terse, moody man, silent when working and not much given to generosity. This was little short of miraculous.

Ezekiel stepped back, allowing Martin to position himself comfortably near the half-completed carving.

He grasped the awl securely in his hand, peered at the fruit closely and with Edric's hand guiding his own lightly, made a careful tap on the end of the awl, allowing the blade to slice cleanly in exactly the right place. Edric took his hand away, and Martin made the second stroke unaided, with perfection. His eyes shone with pride, even on his half- blinded side.

Edric took the tools back from him.

"You are better than you believe, Sir," he told Martin with respect.

Martin left the Abbey walking on air, feeling he had experienced more than one miracle.

William led the lame mare into the stable yard of Wilmington late in the afternoon. It had been a long journey, unable to ride and needing to pace the mare carefully to avoid causing lasting damage to such an expensive beast.

There were few lay brothers in this small priory, but there was one who prided himself on his expertise with horses, and William was fortunate to find him available, willing to look at the mare for a small sum, eager to chat as he ran his hands down the horse's withers.

William sat on an upturned leather bucket, enjoying the ale offered by the man, and eying the few mounts in the stable yard. There were only three other horses; one belonged to the prior, there was a smaller mare for the general use of the good brothers when outside supplies were needed, and the third was a dark chestnut animal with a familiar turn of its head as it tossed its mane.

"Who owns the chestnut mount?"

"A traveller who arrived several days ago in need of help." The reply was guarded; a suspicious look shot William's way.

"I am seeking a traveller with possibly a young child."

There was a silence. The man disappeared into the buttery, returning several moments later with one of the brothers.

"You are enquiring for some-one? May I ask your purpose?"

William explained the long journey, the loss of the child, the young man seeking him - when he mentioned the gang of smugglers the brother held up his hand to stop the flow of talk.

"We are an alien house; we do not concern ourselves with English affairs, but we have heard of such things. I must speak with my prior. Wait here."

Whilst he was waiting, William moved over to the tethered horse, ran a hand over his coat, looked more closely at his marking. He was fairly sure this was Matthias' horse.

The prior came out to speak with William, behind him a tall figure, a rough auburn beard and a head of auburn hair towering over the stately prior.

"Pax et Bonum,"

"Pax et Bonum," William replied, his eyes looking beyond the prior to where Matthias stood.

"Do you know this man?" the prior asked William. He moved to one side to allow William a better look at Matthias.

"I most certainly do!" William answered, relief and joy flooding him. He moved swiftly to embrace Matthias, alarmed at how thin he had become, how much older he looked.

"But what of Luke?" he asked, sharply.

"Come inside. He is recovering but it will take some time," Matthias replied, sombrely.

Before it became too dark, it was decided that William should take Matthias' horse and return to Sir Tobias, leaving the lame horse to rest and return in the morning with the Coroner.

Chapter 14

Alice Stands on Her Own

Alice and Martin planned carefully for the coming marriage feast. Ezekiel and Martha joined in with as much enthusiasm as they could muster, but Ezekiel was more affected than he would admit about the non-appearance of Matthias, and looked eagerly at his boys every day when they returned from the school lest there should be news of him. His leaving Matthias weighed heavily on him; he should have protested and stayed, but he remembered the shepherd boy and knew it would have been impossible.

Lady Bridget, stoical as ever, promised plump chickens for the feast, a gift of fancy fruits from Sherborne market and a cask of good red claret. Elizabeth estimated how much ale they would need to brew, how many manchet loaves to bake and called on Lydia with offers of help in her dress for the day, but to her delight she discovered that several neighbours had taken Lydia's story to their hearts and were planning to weave garlands and stitch her dress from good fabric purchased from Milborne Port market.

Ennis and Freya were becoming excited and animated, having little understanding of the sorrow felt by all. Martin tried to spend more time with Lydia to prepare the home with an extra sleeping place, for Lydia often slept downstairs or in with the two girls.

Ezekiel spoke to Martin about the possibility of bringing his sister Jenna over from Shaftesbury. He thought she would enjoy the opportunity to meet new people, and to see the players on their great cart.

The admiration felt by all when Martin had arrived home with his news that he had actually been invited to leave his mark on one of the misericords was even greater than their delighted response as he told them about his mini miracle in the Abbey when his blinded eye had cleared a little. Martin was sorry that Matthias was not there to share his pleasure, and that knowledge tainted the pleasure, made him feel unworthy of having such good fortune, for it had all come about through the kindness of this family.

Merrik came out to visit them, walking the distance from Sherborne. He discussed with Alice and Martin where they could park their great two storeyed cart, and which plays they would like to see. Martin wanted something light-hearted to try and lift the family mood; nothing sad, nothing full of sin and devils. This proved something of a difficulty since most of the available plays were religious, depicting the nativity or the crucifixion. However, Davy recalled seeing Noah's flood when he went to Sherborne, and so it was decided. Merrik's depressive mood manifested itself on all of them, and although they were pleased to have sought him out, they could not afford to sink in his misery. They were pleased when he moved off to seek out suitable lodgings in the village for the players.

Sir Tobias and William moved from Otham Priory the day after William's discovery. There were tears of joy from the Coroner, candles lit, prayers of thanks given. William emphasized how gaunt Matthias looked, how weak Luke still was, but the Coroner was still shocked when he finally saw them.

Matthias had prepared Luke for meeting his grandfather in this place, had attempted to make sure Luke was clean, awake and dressed, but he could not hide the mental scars which were reflected in his eyes.

Matthias had been able to speak with Luke more freely about his ordeal, but he was wise enough to know that it must be led by Luke himself, not by Matthias prodding at painful memories. He worried how Luke was going to cope when they finally reached Barton Holding, for surely boys would want to know details, ignorant of the pain such questioning would hold.

Sir Tobias quizzed Matthias privately about how much he knew of the journey Luke had taken and the death of Walter the Woodman. He was horrified that a child as young as Luke had been forced to walk so far, had seen the sight of Walter's injuries, had been involved with such a ruthless gang. He was determined to seek out the captain of archers to discover whether they had found the gang leaders who would most certainly hang.

With Luke sleeping late the next morning, worn out by the emotional reunion and still sleeping badly, Sir Tobias, William and Matthias conferred together in the refectory, planning how best to proceed. Sir Tobias would have liked to ride after the royal party to ensure that justice was done, but William and Matthias warned him against this action. It could be fraught with danger and more hardship, and would cause extra worry, travel and on whose horse? His own mare was lame in a front leg, and he was hoping that it was mild and rest would cure this sufficiently for her to be still rideable. If she was not, then that gave them an extra concern.

At least Matthias' money problems were solved, for Sir Tobias had come well-armed with silver and could command monies from the royal coffers.

It was with huge regret that Sir Tobias agreed to abandon his desire to follow through with the royal clerks to ensure justice was carried out. He felt white hot anger at their cruelties and hold on so many poor villages along the coast, but he was out of his own area, and family matters had to take precedence.

Matthias was relieved; he knew the Coroner could be stubborn at times, but he had had enough. He was exhausted, homesick and now extremely worried about his scholars, allowing himself to dwell on the affairs of his business. How many scholars had left him, he wondered? How had Alice coped with the fall-out of his absence and the loss of Luke? How would Luke fit back into his life? The child now clung to him at night when the nightmares came, and Matthias had become well used to the pattern and understood how to calm him.

He drew himself back from his musings to concentrate on Sir Tobias. In truth, he was glad someone else was beginning to take the lead and make decisions, for his body and mind were battered and beaten by events.

Sir Tobias was talking about going to Poole by sea. The horses would be in the hold of a cog quite used to carrying horses, which would mean just a short ride from Wilmington, a sea voyage of possibly four or five days, and a ride from Poole to their home.

They would be home by the middle of the month.

Merrik tried to look forward rather than back. He returned to Sherborne, pleased to have been able to procure work for the players, of whom at one time in the not so distant past he had been part, but still rankling about the escape of Walter the Woodman, perpetrator of hideous murder and the catalyst for his sister's execution.

His frequent forays into the Abbey calmed his mind; he often crouched on the stone floor, his back against a pillar, and simply watched the work, preferring above all to observe Edric.

Edric was accustomed to his presence; watching him seemed all Merrik was content to do, and Edric, himself a silent man, had no objection to the big man's presence.

The players gathered in Sherborne as the October days went by, persuading Merrik to take on the role of Noah as he had done previously. Merrik felt reluctant to do so, aware of his own depression and gloom, but they wore him down eventually, and Merrik found the preparation therapeutic to a certain degree. He found himself beginning to look to the future, uncertain though it might be. Perhaps he should stay with the players - Christmas-tide would be approaching soon and there was always work for mummers and their cart to entertain the gentry in their houses.

He wanted to be around when the Coroner returned, - he hoped he might return with Walter bound hand and foot so justice could truly be done, but so far there was no word of Sir Tobias.

After a further week spent at Wilmington priory, Sir Tobias decided the party should attempt to return home. Luke's bodily scars had healed; the mental scars would take longer, but the ministrations of the kindly brothers were helping. The concoctions of herbs that burned nightly in the little cell some-times calmed him, and bit by bit, fragments of the nightmare were relayed to Matthias, increasingly now a little more calmly. The shuddering sobbing had decreased, and Luke's voice had returned.

Matthias wondered whether it might be wise to attempt to reassure him that Titus' predictions on Luke's future place in the family were unfounded, but decided against it. It didn't seem appropriate at this time, and Luke appeared to cling to Matthias for comfort in a way which made such discussions seem unnecessary.

The party were preparing to depart with the blessing of the Prior. Luke was mounted in front of Matthias, and Sir Tobias' mare was much recovered although would not withstand a long journey; they had planned to ride only as far as Lewes and take ship to Poole.

Before they finally left, Sir Tobias sent William down to Pevensey Haven to reward Angel with a bag of silver. Without Angel and his mother, it was doubtful whether Matthias would have been able to save Luke from being bundled aboard the ship and lost for ever. On William's return he reported that there were soldiers surrounding Pevensey Castle and Angel had told him that the castillion had been arrested and taken away, and certain ships impounded. The village was in uproar and confusion. Sir Tobias had to be content with that, although he privately doubted whether it would prevent the gangs from springing up again. Smuggling was always going to be big business on this part of the coast, but for now, he had done his best to punish those who terrorised the villagers.

There was a weak sun shining as they rode away from Wilmington, joining the main track to Lewes. Their journey was uneventful, passing only traders, travellers, journeymen and one or two merchants. Lewes was a bustling market town which they reached in the late afternoon, and William found a cog which was leaving on the morning tide, willing to take their horses and bound for Shoreham and finally Poole with goods. Like Pevensey Haven, Lewes now had limited shipping, silting up and not so well served with deeper bellied vessels, but they were fortunate in finding this particular one, and before boarding, Sir Tobias insisted on spending money on a new warm cloak for both Luke and Matthias, and boots for Luke whose feet were now sufficiently healed to be able to bear them.

Both Matthias and Sir Tobias were aware that at this time of the year the seas around the coast could be unpredictable, and they fervently hoped they would enjoy a good sea voyage. Luke had not experienced a journey be sea in his short life, and his eyes rounded in terror as they prepared to board, William coaxing the horses up the wooden plank and into the hold.

Matthias remembered how sea-sick he had been on his return from France a few years earlier, and hoped it would not occur again, for he was intent on caring for Luke and didn't wish to find himself a victim of the sea.

In this he was unlucky. The voyage was rough, wind rising even as they set sail. William and Sir Tobias settled down in a corner of the deck, wrapped in their cloaks, and he and Luke crouched miserably near the rail, moaning with sea sickness for the first day. On day two the wind abated a little and Matthias found himself able to sit with his back to the decking, Luke asleep with his head on Matthias' knees. They put in at the port of Shoreham, but it was a different place from the beach on which Walter had met his end. Looking towards the mass of land in the distance, Matthias picked out the soft rise of the South Downs and in his imagination was back on the trail with Ezekiel, pounding along following the pack ponies but never catching them. He shivered as he thought what a narrow escape Luke had had. He couldn't quite take in what distance they had travelled, and he had even lost track of how long they had been away.

The cog battled on through choppy seas the next day, hugging the coastline as far as possible. Luke found his sea legs and was interested in the way the sailors worked, manning the lookout, running up and down with no care for the shifting, heaving, creaking deck. The wind brushed a little colour into his cheeks and Matthias was pleased to see he was even asking questions of one of the sailors.

They put in again at Chichester, and then Southampton, where one or two more passengers came aboard. Southampton was a larger and busier port, and Luke watched bigger vessels unload as they tied up, listening to strange tongues jabbering to each other and unloading new and different goods from further away.

Finally, on day five, they arrived at Poole and William and Sir Tobias disembarked with their horses, paid the captain, and they all made their way to the house of William's sister, who lived just outside Poole. They spent the night there, eating a simple meal, enjoying her home brewed ale and sleeping late on the following morning, ready for the last push home. They would need one more night at Wimborne and then they would make for home.

Three days remained until October twenty eighth, the feast of St. Jude, hope and impossible causes. The players cart was arriving at any time now, together with the cohort of players, and the baking, cleaning and decorating of the barn was well under way. Martin had cleared all his belongings from the barn which had been his home for nearly two years now, and Elizabeth had swept and polished it to make way for the trestle tables on which would be the wedding feast.

Lady Bridget had organized her household into baking, pushing firmly aside her fears for her husband's safety and that of Matthias, her kinsman. She had faced fears concerning the Coroner before; she told herself sternly that she would face them again, but for now concentrate on this day of rejoicing for Martin which Alice had so bravely planned.

Alice wished with all her heart that Matthias was safe somewhere, but her doubts would keep surfacing however hard she tried to ignore them. The false sense of gaiety which pervaded the household was brittle, tinged with sadness for those missing from the festivities. She found it hard to comprehend that she would not hold her child in her arms again, nor experience the intimacy of her husband's touch on her body. When she allowed herself to dwell on those thoughts, she felt physically sick and wondered how she could go through with her plans.

The scholars were building up to a crescendo of excitement; they had come to admire Martin's perseverance, his willing acceptance of his disabilities, and they were full of wonderment at his experience in the Abbey. They and their families were all invited to the feast, and Martin and Alice had made sure that they understood the story which was to be told by the mummers.

Although some people in the village when they learned of it were convinced it was a miracle and would have made much of it, Martin was bold enough to assure them that it was not a miracle, - just the stretching of his neck, the movement of his eye that had unlocked something.

Alice sometimes wondered what Matthias would say if he returned and found Martin gone and his beloved school expanded with one or two girls included in his scholars, but she knew that would be a bridge to cross if it ever happened.

Chapter 15

A Homecoming

Ezekiel was on his way to collect Jenna from the great nunnery at Shaftesbury. He had allowed himself time to call on Master Croxhale at the Swan, for that was where they had left Luke's poor pony, all those weeks ago. Ezekiel thought it was time he collected the pony and returned it to Alice; Jenna could ride him as they travelled back to Milborne Port for Martin and Lydia's wedding.

He thought about Matthias a great deal now, sorry that he had not been able to remain with him, for surely there was safety in numbers. What had happened to him, and when would Sir Tobias return? There were cases piling up for him in Sherborne; the sheriff would not be delighted with him if he did not return soon. He himself owed Jenna's life to Matthias; Martin's fortunes were in a large part due to the kindness of Matthias; his two young sons were now part of Matthias' school, so he owed their education to Matthias - the list went on, so what had happened to Matthias?

He reached The Swan and made himself known to John Croxhale. The pony looked different after many weeks recuperating with the landlord. He had put on weight and his coat had returned to its former glossy state. Ezekiel insisted on paying for the care he had shown and left the inn to collect his sister.

They travelled slowly together, relishing the feeling of family and looking forward to the coming festivities, but both brother and sister returned time and time again to wondering what had befallen Matthias. Ezekiel rarely touched on the subject of Isaac her late husband with Jenna, content that Jenna's wounds had healed; she was nearly back to her old self and her speech and memory were improved every time he saw her.

There were travellers on the road; some merchants, a few pedlars with packs, - one even had a little monkey on a strap which Jenna looked at curiously as they overtook them.

They were nearing Henstridge where two paths crossed, one leading to Stalbridge and the other, on which they were travelling, led ultimately to Exeter, taking in Sherborne. Ezekiel watched as a party of three horsemen pulled out well in front of them from the cross-track to join the main route.

He and Jenna would catch up with them very soon, for they were travelling slowly. It looked to Ezekiel as if one of the horsemen had something awkward mounted in front of him, which might account for their lack of speed. He hoped it did not mean a sick traveller – the plague years were behind them, but the wet Summer and now damp Autumn encouraged sickness of all kinds.

They drew nearer, Ezekiel keeping an eye on the party ahead, for they could not know whether the horsemen were honest travellers or rogues waiting to ambush others on the road. He slowed his horse to a walk, and as he did so, the party in front of them also slowed to a stop, causing Ezekiel to draw his blade from its sheath.

He screwed his eyes to see better why they had stopped, observing one rider dismount and lift something from his horse. Another rider dismounted, looking back towards them, and Ezekiel tightened his grip on the knife.

"Do exactly as I say, Jenna," he muttered. "We may have trouble ahead."

He urged his steed into a canter, Jenna following him closely. Ezekiel intended to gather speed and overtake them, rushing past them at speed whilst the two riders were still standing, but one of them stood in the middle of the track, hands held out, palms facing in a gesture of peace.

Ezekiel pulled his mount up so swiftly that Jenna was nearly thrown as she tried to imitate her brother.

Sir Tobias lowered his hands as they came closer to him, and Ezekiel recognized him suddenly, shouting out gladly in welcome.

He looked closely at the other rider standing beside Sir Tobias - thinner than he had been the last time Ezekiel had seen him, but hollow eyed with a frail child....

"Matthias!" he gasped. "We feared you dead! God be praised! And Luke...Luke...."

Emotion overcame him and he fell on Matthias' neck, sobbing with relief and joy. Jenna smiled nervously at the sight of her brother so overcome, causing William to move his horse closer to her for reassurance.

Sir Tobias found tears trickling down his cheeks as he embraced Luke, lifting him in his arms, secretly appalled at how light and fragile he seemed.

The conjoined party now paused by the track-side to exchange immediate news, sobs, cries of surprise, gasps of relief from everyone except Luke, who was strangely quiet. He stayed close to Matthias, needing his closeness to face up to the excitement.

"Luke, let me have you in front of me - give Matthias a rest to ride alone," suggested the Coroner.

He was disappointed when Luke shook his head and clung to Matthias, but an exchange of looks between the two men settled it, Luke remaining with Matthias.

The rest of the ride passed as in a dream for all. Matthias indicated that the story had best wait until later, but Ezekiel was delighted to be able to explain why Jenna was with them, that tomorrow Martin and Lydia would be wed and the festivities were all in hand at Barton Holding, thanks to Lady Alice.

Matthias found his cheeks aching with the attempt to smile and appear glad. In truth he was glad for Martin – very glad indeed, for Martin so deserved to be happy after all that had befallen him; how, Matthias wondered, did that now affect his own relationship with Alice? It very much sounded as if she had progressed without him exceedingly well, organizing a wedding feast, finding players, offering accommodation for Jenna and other guests, including the scholars in the festivities to come. Matthias had looked forward so much to his return with Luke, the apple of his wife's eye - was this to be overshadowed by new directions in his absence?

As Ezekiel chattered on, oblivious of his friend's unease, Matthias tried to school himself to accept this new state of affairs, but he worried about how Luke would be able to cope with the crowds, the festivities, the rich food, the hustle. He had tried to prepare Luke whilst on the journey, remembering individual friends, talking about his nursemaid Lindy, remembering Martin's delicate carvings...and Luke had started to respond; there was the beginning of a spark in his eyes, but it was a slow beginning. Was all that going to be washed away in the frenetic homecoming on the eve of a wedding feast?

Alice paused to look at what she had put on the walls of the barn. Martin had cleared all his belongings out and Davy had helped him transport them to Lydia's. She had been up and out early with Elizabeth collecting greenery, - ivy, berried twigs, even some golden leaves from the hedgerows, for the Autumn colours still held their glow, despite the persistent rain. The barn was starting to resemble a festive place, waiting for Davy to bring the two trestles in on which they would place the food tomorrow.

She was pleased with the effects of their work, but she did so wish Matthias could see how she had managed. Surely he would not still consider her spoilt? She tried not to think of her son, for that had indeed left an ache, a hole in her life which could never be filled. There was a chance that Matthias might still be alive - hadn't her father ridden off to gather news - but a child, gone so long...no...there seemed no hope there.

Martin and Lydia were breathless with excitement and gratitude at the villagers' gift to them. It seemed that they had really taken Martin's story to heart, and within the space of two days, a stone construction, neatly built, with a hard packed earthen floor and a roof of thatched reeds had been added to the back of the humble downstairs room, more than adequate for the double bed given by Sir Tobias and Lady Bridget. The work had been organized by several men of the village, all competent at constructing simple walls and adding a roof which would keep out rain as well.

Martin's greatest sorrow of course was the disappearance of Matthias, to whom he owed this happiness, and the child Luke, who had watched him work so many times, sitting cross legged on the floor, silently enjoying his presence.

Davy and Elizabeth had worked hard alongside Lady Alice, not just for this day, but to keep the household and the school running smoothly, but as the days turned into weeks, and now into months, they had cause to wonder how it would all end.

The players' great cart was parked in the meadow, sufficiently near to the barn to allow guests to run for shelter if the rain squalled as it was wont to do recently, although today was a clearer day. Merrik stayed with the cart and all the props and costumes overnight, making himself comfortable in the cart, whilst the company of players would arrive from Sherborne on the morrow, ready to set up their play for the evening after the wedding feast.

Alice and her mother completed the decoration of the barn, checked the progress in the kitchen, where Elizabeth had the loan of one of Lady Bridget's serving girls and ascended the stairs to the solar upstairs to discuss arrangements for the following day.

As they sat, two ladies relaxing together under their individual strained circumstances, they heard the sound of hooves in the yard.

Alice rose and peered out of the small glazed window of the solar. A loan horseman was dismounting.

"It looks like Ezekiel!" she exclaimed, with a slight frown, "but where is Jenna? He rode to Shaftesbury to collect Jenna."

They heard the clatter of boots on the floor beneath them as he entered the house. Alice couldn't catch the words, but it was obviously a request to see her, for Elizabeth knocked on the solar door and ushered Ezekiel in, withdrawing and closing the door behind her.

"What is it? What is the matter?" Lady Bridget cried, suddenly fearful as Ezekiel stood silently before them. Her hand went to her heart and she staggered and would have fallen had Alice not caught her mother.

Ezekiel lowered her back onto the chair she had occupied and tried to speak coherently.

"Nothing is the matter - nothing at all. Compose yourselves as I have not been able to do – I am come ahead to warn you – we have encountered strangers on the road – "

Alice did not let him finish. "Strangers? With news of my husband and my son? My father, too?"

"Strangers indeed," Ezekiel continued. "A Coroner and his squire..."

"My husband and William – "

"and more – but needing some careful greeting, I think. A rider with a head of auburn hair, and in front of him mounted on the same horse, my Lady Alice, your son, Luke."

Alice stood and would have rushed from the room, but Ezekiel put out his hand to stop her, catching the sleeve of her gown.

"Wait, Lady. This is why I have come ahead. Luke is silent, thin, has been in the darkest of places. Matthias looks haunted, exhausted and years older. Whatever they have endured has not been told yet, but Matthias is concerned that the exultant welcome which Luke will have from yourself, My Lady, will undo the relative calm he has managed to achieve. He begs restraint and a quiet place for the reunion."

Alice controlled herself at once.

"Of course, Ezekiel. What do you suggest? How should we do this?"

"They will be nearly here now. May I suggest that you both greet them in the yard where they dismount. Let Martin know to keep the scholars inside – it is not yet time for them to ride home – and ask Matthias to carry Luke to his own room? Then you can sit with them in privacy."

Alice hastened to the schoolroom where Martin was working with the scholars, but imparting the news to Martin was harder than she thought it would be. She was shaking so much that her voice was uneven, and when his face lit up at the news, she was sure the scholars would suspect and want to rush out and cheer. However, she wanted to do as Matthias had directed, and Martin quickly understood that events might not be quite as exuberant as they would all have liked.

The little party rounded the rise leading down to the house; Matthias' heart jumped as he saw his own house once more. The barn was wide open, doors pinned back unusually, for whilst Martin had lived there the closed doors had given him both privacy and security.

He saw Alice first, blue gown which he had always liked so much helping him to pick her out at a distance, and beside her, Lady Bridget, her hands linked with Alice.

She came towards them as they entered the yard and as Matthias' hands weakly dropped the reins, Alice took them without a word and led the horse nearer to the mounting block. He looked speechlessly at her before lifting Luke into her waiting arms.

She gathered Luke to her, holding him close and waited until Matthias had dismounted. Her clear blue eyes met Matthias' green ones.

"Welcome home," she breathed softly.

Davy appeared silently from the kitchen to take the horse away, and as Sir Tobias and William dismounted, Ezekiel came to Jenna to assist her.

Matthias, Alice and Luke disappeared into the house together, leaving Lady Bridget to propel the remaining party into the solar.

Matthias and Alice joined the party in the solar shortly, leaving Luke in his own room, mercifully fast asleep. Martin was invited and Davy and Elizabeth crowded in at Matthias' instruction, for he had never left them out of his plans or information, having their total trust and loyalty.

"He will not sleep long, nor restfully," Matthias warned.

Ezekiel had already told the beginning of the journey, how they had picked up the pony in Shaftesbury with news of Walter's intentions, how they had travelled to Salisbury, Southampton, and then on to the tracks used by the pack ponies, had met the young shepherd lad Ralph and then been followed by the two men who had mistaken them for King's tax men, evading them purely by chance. How they had then taken the decision for Ezekiel to return after Ralph had warned them of the ruthless nature of such gangs, taking Ralph with him and for Matthias to travel on alone, hoping to catch up with them before Walter had the opportunity to sell Luke.

Matthias found his tired mind could not tell the story with too much clarity, almost as if now it was over he failed to remember the details. He closed his eyes, trying to recall the wet, windy weather, the exhaustion of his horse, the lack of food and water, how closely he had to watch the money for he knew he did not have an unlimited amount, the despair in his heart as the days had grown shorter, wetter, colder. Then the discovery of Luke, assistance from Angel being so like a divine stroke of genius, how Luke and he had scrambled up the cliff, desperate to avoid the smugglers gang, Luke clinging to his back.

A wild scream interrupted his tale. Swiftly he rose even as Alice did, and went to Luke's bedside. Alice tried to take him in her arms but to her dismay Luke beat her off with his bony fists, screaming and sobbing. She recoiled in distress. Matthias picked the child up, murmuring softly to him, holding his flailing hands, stroking his face, pacing the floor with Luke in his arms.

The child quietened, weeping softly but allowed Matthias to put him back in his bed. Matthias remained by the bed humming quietly and Luke slipped back into an uneasy slumber.

"I'm sorry, Alice," Matthias murmured, aware of her shocked face. "This will happen several times more before the night is over. I have calmed him many nights, but I'm afraid it seems no one else can."

"Teach me how to do it, Matthias. Show me how to reach my son. You need sleep also."

"I will try, Alice. Luke and I have been through days of hell together. It has something to do with that."

"My days have been hell too, Matthias. I thought I had lost my husband as well as my son."

"Never, Alice. We are home. Luke will heal."

"Are you healed, Matthias?"

"How could I not be when I look at you, Alice."

He opened his arms to her, stiff and weary with days of travel, and she folded herself gently against his body.

"Thank you for my son, Matthias. My family is home now."

The sun shone on Lydia and Martin's nuptials. Matthias had slept fitfully, leaving their bed several times during the night to calm Luke, Alice knowing she must accept this for now. It was a small price to pay for their safe return.

Martin felt his cup would overflow with joy on this day. Ennis and Freya were now part of his family, he had earned the respect of many villagers, he was a part of something good – he would never have thought that possible when he first crawled into this village, seeking the Coroner's daughter with news of her husband's death.

Merrik heard of their return and the Coroner gave him a full account of the doings and death of Walter the Woodman.

Merrik felt very responsible for the terrible things Luke had seen and experienced, but his loss from Walter's evil life was great, and he could not yet expunge the guilt he experienced for his sister's death. Walter had been a malevolent influence in their lives, and he needed cleansing.

After his brilliant performance as Noah on the player's cart, which was hugely enjoyed by all, Merrik sat watching the dying days of the wedding feast.

Martin and Lydia had been carried off by the villagers. Over-excited and tired, Freya and Ennis were looked after by some neighbours to give them privacy for their first night of wedded bliss, with many nods and winks from the over indulged village boys.

The Coroner and his family had departed, together with Ezekiel, Martha and their boys. Jenna went with them, but not before Merrik had sought her out, liking the look of this quiet, serious featured lady, who, he discovered, was widowed. He had a mind to see more of her before she returned to Shaftesbury. Perhaps this place was a lucky place for people – it was time he had some luck.

Matthias' household fell into the house when all guests had left, Alice proud of the way the day had gone, delighted at the pleasure Martin and Lydia had experienced at all points of the day. The scholars had taken to heart what Matthias had told them and had quietly hugged Luke and then left him alone, and Luke himself had sat watchful, keeping close to Matthias whenever possible, and now was sleeping, although for how long Matthias was unsure.

What he was sure of however, was that he was home where he belonged, where Luke belonged, where Alice belonged, and where they could now at last move forward as a family.

Chapter 16

.....and a Future

At the turn of the year Luke finally felt able to resume his place in the schoolroom. His recovery had been slow, gradual, much helped by his new relationship with Matthias. He did not talk much to the other scholars about his experiences, preferring to keep them between himself and Matthias, and although curious, the scholars were obedient to Matthias' demands, and allowed Luke to slip back into his place within the school. Alice and Matthias had visited Thomas Copeland to defer his place in Sherborne for a further year, and Thomas, on hearing details which horrified him, agreed readily that it was the right thing to do.

Sir Tobias was unable to let the smuggling band rest. Although not within his jurisdiction, he sent messengers to the king, requesting information on the outcome of their troubles, and received return messages with details including names of prominent leaders, several of whom were well born young lords, intent on building power houses for themselves, making use of the unrest in Sussex and Kent.

Daily conditions of the poor were such that it was not difficult to find followers who had been promised riches and prosperity. There had been hangings in both Sussex and Kent.

Sir Tobias remained deeply perturbed by the unrest in the country as a whole, and with his experience and wisdom, could foresee troubled times ahead of them when the Yorks and the Lancasters finally met head to head, as he was convinced they would.

Meanwhile, he thought, enjoy the peace of Dorset for the moment. He attempted to discover more details of Walter the Woodman, but in this he was unsuccessful, the Sheriff of the area declaring the case closed. Sir Tobias was not happy with his decision, but Merrik felt it would serve no purpose to pursue the matter, so regretfully, as an honest Coroner and Justice of the Peace, Sir Tobias allowed the matter to drop.

Merrik remained a member of the travelling players, enjoying their programme of events during the Christmas period, and finding time to visit the carvings in the Abbey. He still found deep peace when watching Edric, whose work progressed slowly, such was the intricate and delicate nature of his skill.

Jenna accompanied him once or twice, staying with Ezekiel and Martha over the festive period. Jenna found a safety in Merrik's presence, and Merrik watched over her with careful affection. He began to plan more visits with her whenever he could, finding her an antidote to his gloom.

Martin and Lydia had found a niche in the life of the village, Ennis now being a full time member of Matthias' school, much to Alice's delight. In gratitude for his work whilst Matthias was absent, Matthias did not charge Ennis any fees, and planned to introduce at least one other girl, should anyone suitable enquire. Martin watched the transformation of the barn with interest; the school was expanding yet again, and he wondered whether he would be invited to help in the future.

In the early Spring, Matthias sought Martin out one morning.

"Are you able to bring yourself to the school during the mornings for a little while?" he asked.

Martin looked quizzically at Matthias.

"Don't tell me...Alice is sick in the mornings?"

Matthias nodded, a smile lighting up his face.

"At last!"

Martin struggled to stand to hug him tightly.

"Does Luke know and understand?" he asked.

"We have not excluded him from anything, "Matthias told him.

Martin watched Matthias leave with a spring in his step and felt nothing but gladness for his friend.

A new chapter had opened in all their lives, although the next few years would open divisions in the kingdom, which would surely touch these innocent people, forcing them into decisions which would affect their very existence.

For now, however, peace and serenity reigned supreme.

Author's notes

The beautiful carvings in Sherborne Abbey under the choir stalls, known as misericords, can be seen on a visit to the Abbey. They were carved in or around the time of 1450 – 1500 and were intended to offer the monks some ease when singing their nightly offices, standing up. The word "misericord" means mercy, so these were mercy seats, affording the monks mercy from the agony of standing whilst singing their offices.

Although much of this book deals with matters away from Sherborne tracing an imaginary trail of wool smugglers along the South Coast, Sherborne Abbey is very much in the background as a stabling influence on their lives.

There were and still are smuggling gangs working the coast of England, and wool was a valuable commodity in 1440 – and it is certainly true that there were taxes on wool which went directly to the King. Wool was needed in England by this time, as well as in the low countries. Weavers were coming to England and the cloth trade here was growing, meaning there was less wool to export.

Violence and quick death were a feature of medieval life. Most people had access to knives and were prepared to use them, but Walter the Woodman had evil thoughts brought about by traumatic scenes from his own life – much the same as happens today in some cases.

Communication is so easy today that it is hard to realise that with no means of a quick text, once Matthias and Ezekiel were away, no-one would know where they were or for how long they would be gone. A good horse could travel between

15 – 20 miles a day, weather permitting. Some rivers, such as those in Sussex have now silted up so no harbours still exist there. Pevensey and Lewes are two such, but Shoreham is still a very active port, and as children, we used to use a beach to the West of the harbour called The Wide Water, where there was a little church called the church of the Good Shepherd. This is the beach on which Walter was killed.

The King, Henry VI, never did take full control of the country, preferring instead to rely on his advisers, some of whom supported the Duke of York, and some of whom supported the Duke of Lancaster, which led ultimately, a few years further down the line, to the Wars of the Roses.

De la Pole, Duke of Suffolk, was one of his chief advisors, constantly arguing with Bishop Beaufort, and Sir Tobias did meet Suffolk on his visit to the court at Windsor.

Suffolk, together with Bishop Ayscough, Bishop of Salisbury and confessor to the king, met untimely ends a few years later – very much the stuff of stories – and this will feature in the final book of the Sherborne Medieval mysteries.